He Was A Very Persuasive Man…Many A Woman Could Attest To That….

The kiss had been a part of a carefully crafted plan of seduction, and she'd walked right into his trap without a moment's hesitation.

"We'll forget what just happened."

He backed up a few steps, "Go ahead and try to forget it."

"We need to maintain a professional relationship."

"Selene, I didn't hire you. Ella did. As far as I'm concerned, you work for her, not me. Which means we don't have a professional relationship."

Without responding, Selene turned, and sprinted down the narrow steps to the safety of her bedroom. No doubt about it, Adrien Morrell had cast his spell over Selene. Now it was up to her to break free, before she, too, found herself caught in the clutches of obsession and allowed him to do anything he pleased.

Dear Reader,

Thanks for choosing Silhouette Desire this month. We have a delectable selection of reads for you to enjoy, beginning with our newest installment of THE ELLIOTTS. *Mr. and Mistress* by Heidi Betts is the story of millionaire Cullen Elliott and his mistress who is desperately trying to hide her unexpected pregnancy. Also out this month is the second book of Maureen Child's SUMMER OF SECRETS. *Strictly Lonergan's Business* is a boss/assistant book that will delight you all the way through to its wonderful conclusion.

We are launching a brand-new continuity series this month with SECRET LIVES OF SOCIETY WIVES. The debut title, *The Rags-To-Riches Wife* by Metsy Hingle, tells the story of a working-class woman who has a night of passion with a millionaire and then gets blackmailed into becoming his wife.

We have much more in store for you this month, including Merline Lovelace's *Devlin and the Deep Blue Sea,* part of her cross-line series, CODE NAME: DANGER, in which a feisty female pilot becomes embroiled in a passionate, dangerous relationship. Brenda Jackson is back with a new unforgettable Westmoreland male, in *The Durango Affair.* And Kristi Gold launches a three-book thematic promotion about RICH AND RECLUSIVE men, with *House of Midnight Fantasies.*

Please enjoy all the wonderful books we have for you this month in Silhouette Desire.

Happy reading,

Melissa Jeglinski

Melissa Jeglinski
Senior Editor
Silhouette Books

Please address questions and book requests to:
Silhouette Reader Service
U.S.: 3010 Walden Ave., P.O. Box 1325, Buffalo, NY 14269
Canadian: P.O. Box 609, Fort Erie, Ont. L2A 5X3

KRISTI GOLD

House
of Midnight
Fantasies

Published by Silhouette Books
America's Publisher of Contemporary Romance

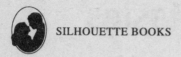

SILHOUETTE BOOKS

ISBN 0-373-76728-5

HOUSE OF MIDNIGHT FANTASIES

Printed in U.S.A.

Books by Kristi Gold

Silhouette Desire

Cowboy for Keeps #1308
Doctor for Keeps #1320
His Sheltering Arms #1350
Her Ardent Sheikh #1358
**Dr. Dangerous* #1415
**Dr. Desirable* #1421
**Dr. Destiny* #1427
His E-Mail Order Wife #1454
The Sheikh's Bidding #1485
**Renegade Millionaire* #1497
Marooned with a Millionaire #1517
Expecting the Sheikh's Baby #1531
Fit for a Sheikh #1576
Challenged by the Sheikh #1586
†*Persuading the Playboy King* #1600
†*Unmasking the Maverick*
    Prince #1606
†*Daring the Dynamic Sheikh* #1612
Mistaken for a Mistress #1669
A Most Shocking Revelation #1695
House of Midnight Fantasies #1728

*Marrying an M.D.
†The Royal Wager

KRISTI GOLD

admits to having a fondness for major league baseball, double cheese enchiladas and creating dark and somewhat dangerous—albeit honorable—heroes. She considers indulging in all three in the same day as the next best thing to a beach vacation!

Kristi resides in central Texas with her retired physician husband and the occasional guest in the form of one of her three grown children. She loves to hear from readers and can be contacted through her Web site at http://kristigold.com or through snail mail at 6902 Woodway Drive, #166, Waco, TX 76712 (Please include SASE for response).

To my good friend and fellow author
Karen Rose Smith. A heartfelt thanks for your gentle
guidance and unwavering support.

One

Maison de Minuit. The House of Midnight.

The name alone seemed ominous, but the forbidding Louisiana plantation symbolized Selene Albright Winston's first serious step toward freedom.

Gathering her courage, Selene left her sedan, apprehension shadowing every step while she walked the flagstone path that led to the lengthy porch. Not even the whisper of a wind ruffled the leaves and only the occasional sound of a cicada disturbed the eerie silence. Ancient gnarled-finger oaks, dripping with Spanish moss, covered the lawns like sinister sentries warding off intruders. The tall grass held a cast of brown and a spattering of milkweeds, and no flowers adorned the overgrown beds lined with withering hedges.

She stopped a few feet from the porch to study the house that seemed as if it had been abandoned, too. In many ways it had, at least superficially. The Greek

Revival mansion's pale yellow facade showed definite signs of aging, and so did the shutters, trim and the six massive columns supporting the structure—all oddly painted as black as the entry sign. She hoped the interior had fared better than the exterior, otherwise not even the most curious person would dare step foot in this place. In fact, turning around and heading for safety was Selene's initial instinct. Not this time. Safety also came with a price.

When she ascended the first wooden stair leading to the entry, it groaned as if it might buckle. Yet the abrupt assault on her psyche proved to be much more disturbing.

Eyes. Ice blue eyes. Intense eyes.

Selene closed her mind as well as her own eyes against the image until it disappeared. But when she scaled the second step, the vision came back, stealing her breath and her confidence. She refused to let this happen. Refused to invite this into her world, not when she had tried so hard for years to keep it reined in.

She drew in a deep breath and raised the invisible mental shield she'd developed for self-protection, relieved to discover it didn't fail her when she took the third and final step onto the porch.

After only a slight hesitation, she rapped on the peeling black door then smoothed a hand down her tailored sleeveless red dress. Though the fabric was lightweight, she felt as if she were wearing a winter parka. She'd pulled her hair back into a band low at her nape, yet that, too, provided little relief from the relentless June heat. Of course, a solid case of nerves contributed to her discomfort, and so did the fact that no one answered her summons.

She knocked one more time, both relieved and anxious when she heard the sound of approaching footsteps. She had no idea who might be on the other side of the door. No idea if she would find friend or foe—or maybe even the owner of the disturbing eyes.

The door finally opened to a woman with keen dark eyes who appeared to be in her sixties, her black-and-silver hair styled in a short, severe cut. She wore a loose-fitting pale green shift and a guarded expression, but she didn't appear to be at all threatening. "May I help you?" she asked in a soft voice that contrasted with her sharp features.

"Are you Ms. Lanoux?" Selene asked.

"Yes, and you are?"

At least Selene was in the right place, even if the woman didn't seem to have a clue as to why she was there. "Selene Winston. I'm here about the restoration."

The woman's hand fluttered to her hair. "I wasn't expecting you until tomorrow."

When they'd spoken last Friday, Selene could have sworn they'd agreed she would interview for the job on Monday. Maybe she should return to the local inn where she'd been residing for the past ten days since her spontaneous escape from Georgia. Maybe she should consider this misunderstanding as a Do Not Enter sign. "If it's not a good time, I can come back tomorrow."

"I wouldn't hear of it," she said as she stepped aside and gestured Selene forward. "Welcome to *Maison de Minuit*... It's Mrs. Winston, isn't it?"

"Winston's my married name, but I'm divorced." Selene internally flinched over the bitterness that resonated in her tone. "Actually, I'd rather you call me Selene."

The woman thankfully maintained a pleasant demeanor. "And you may call me Ella. Now let's get you out of the heat."

When Selene stepped inside the wide foyer, she immediately noticed two things—the house wasn't much cooler than the porch outside, and the light was all but filtered out by heavy shutters covering the windows. A gloomy atmosphere encompassed the area, along with the scent of aged wood and musty air.

She followed Ella down the vestibule where they paused at a small parlor that proved to be as dark as the entrance, any natural light blocked by thick blue drapes. The Federal-style antiques set about the room were most likely original furnishings, and worth a fortune, Selene decided. Nothing she hadn't seen—or owned—in her former life. A life she had gladly left behind. Still, she'd always had an affinity for all things historical, and the pieces were definitely worth investigating.

"This is only one of the common areas," Ella said. "And like the rest of the house, it needs refurbishing." She fanned her face in a rapid succession of waves. "Inside and out. You would have to obtain estimates on a new cooling system and most likely a new roof, which means you'll have to find a suitable contractor."

"Wait a minute," Selene said as soon as the woman's words registered. "I had no idea the job would be quite this extensive."

"My dear, you can hire anyone you'd like," Ella said. "Unless you have a problem supervising workers."

In reality, no, Selene didn't. She'd managed a household staff for years. Besides, she had nowhere else to be. No place to go aside from her former home, and that wasn't an option. "I can handle it, as long as I have a substantial budget to follow."

"Money is no object."

Obviously Ella Lanoux had sufficient wealth even though she wasn't at all like the well-heeled matrons Selene had known most of her life, including her own mother. Although Selene wasn't exactly comfortable with the magnitude of the restoration, she had to remember why she'd come here—to seek employment. To be her own person, make her own money. To start over.

Ella brushed her damp bangs from her forehead, then motioned Selene forward. "Follow me and we'll continue the tour." She strode down the foyer, stopped at a set of double doors and faced Selene again. "This is by far the most impressive part of the house."

With dramatic flair, Ella threw open the doors to reveal a massive circular room covered in what appeared to be original wood-plank floors. In the center of that room, a freestanding, wide red-carpeted staircase spiraled to the second floor. Selene's gaze tracked to the ceiling that showcased gold-winged cherubs flitting about a large expanse of cloud-bedecked blue sky, a chandelier dripping with crystals serving as the focal point. She'd seen this type of room before, but only in photographs that couldn't compare to witnessing the real thing with her own eyes. "This is absolutely breathtaking."

Ella smiled proudly. "It had that effect on me the first time I saw it." She pointed across the way. "The kitchen and dining room are through there. We can see those later. I'll show you the second floor now."

As she followed Ella up the stairway, her hand firmly gripping the white iron railing, Selene felt as if she were climbing toward heaven. A tranquil piece of paradise among the darkness.

When they reached the landing, Ella stopped and nodded to her left. "That corridor leads to the front of the house where you'll find two rooms. One was formerly a nursery, the other's been converted into a private office."

Heavy emphasis on *private*, Selene noted. She motioned to her right. "And down that way?"

"The rest of the second-floor bedrooms, including where you'll be staying if we come to an agreement."

"I would be expected to live on-site?"

"Room and board would be included while you're here."

Selene supposed it would make things more convenient. She wouldn't have to drive the ten miles or so into town, or find a suitable place to live. *If* she decided to accept the job. A decision not to be taken lightly, Selene thought as she trailed behind Ella, who made an immediate right into a narrow paneled hallway illuminated by the occasional dimly lit lamp mounted to the wall.

They'd only walked a few feet when Selene's attention landed straight ahead on a bronze life-size statue looming at the end of the corridor. A demonic creature complete with horns, pointy teeth and claws with a terrified, scantily clad woman in its grasp. The menacing figure definitely contrasted with the angels keeping watch over the rotunda downstairs. A classic illustration of good versus evil. Heaven opposed to hell.

Selene suddenly found herself in the grip of another vision. Unlike her first images on the entry steps, this came to her as if she were watching somewhere on the sidelines, as it always had in the past. The image of a hand sliding down her bare arm. A very large, very male hand that continued down her back, formed to her waist, drifted to her bottom, before she blinked and forced the image away. She had no idea where the vision had originated since there seemed to be no one around. And she found that more than a little troublesome.

She hadn't realized she'd come to a complete stop until Ella turned and favored her with another smile. "It's rather grotesque, isn't it? I call him Giles, after the former owner. The crazy man loved that thing, but then he was always known for being eccentric."

Eccentric wouldn't be the term Selene used to describe the former owner. *Scary* would be more like it. She couldn't imagine wanting the "thing" around every morning, or at bedtime. "I'm surprised he didn't take it with him." She was sorry he hadn't.

Ella laughed. "Unfortunately, it was too big to fit in his coffin."

Selene internally cringed. Was that the source of her vision—the mental musings of a ghost? That had never happened to her before. Normally she channeled the thoughts of living, breathing humans, at her own peril at certain points in her life. "I'm sorry to hear he passed away."

"Don't be," Ella said. "He was almost ninety and quite frankly, I thought he was too cantankerous to die. In fact, he had a mistress forty years his junior. She's the one who did him in."

"She killed him?" Selene couldn't disguise her distress.

Ella shook her head and laughed again. "Not intentionally. Let's just say the Morrell men have virility down to a fine art. Unfortunately, Giles didn't know his limitations."

"Well, at least he left this world a happy man." Now for the question foremost on Selene's mind. "Did he pass away in this house?"

"No. He died in France." Selene's frame relaxed from relief until Ella added, "But unfortunately, this place has a reputation for tragedy."

Great. Just what Selene wanted to hear—the mansion could be home to restless spirits intent on haunting her brain. But only if she let that happen, which she wouldn't, if she could prevent it.

They continued on for a few steps until Ella stopped at a closed door. "Your quarters would be in here." She pointed toward the end of the hallway where the demon held court. "That guest room over there is closed for the time being. The current owner keeps it locked and prefers it not be disturbed."

Selene gaped for a few moments. "I thought you were the owner."

Ella frowned. "Oh, dear, I'm sorry if I gave you that impression. Adrien Morrell, Giles's grandson, inherited the plantation. I'm his assistant." Her frown melted into a cynical smile. "And his maid and cook. I also advise him from time to time, whether he asks for my advice or not."

Selene was beginning to suspect she had a lot to learn, and worried some of it might not be pleasant at all. "Does Mr. Morrell live here?" she asked.

"That's his room." Ella indicated a closed door nearby. "It's the master suite and adjacent to your room, but I promise he won't bother you."

"Where is your room?" Selene asked.

"Off the kitchen. I spend much of my time there. And this would be your room." Ella opened the door to the prospective living quarters and waved Selene inside.

As it was with the rest of the house, the bedroom was adorned with more antiques, including a huge cherry-wood Victorian double bed covered in a white lace spread. Several colorful braided rugs covered the hardwood floors that had lost their sheen. Straight ahead, the white curtains were pulled back to reveal double French doors opening to a veranda that apparently faced the back of the heavily wooded property. Several fans were set about the room, including two overhead, but they did little to alleviate the heat.

"I'm afraid it doesn't have a private bath," Ella said. "You would have to use the one across the hall that serves this wing."

Now that was just wonderful, sharing a bathroom with a total stranger. And a man, no less. Of course, she'd shared a bath with a virtual stranger before—her husband. And toward the end of the marriage, Richard had slept in another bedroom altogether. Lived in his own private world. A world that hadn't included his wife. "Then I assume that means Mr. Morrell uses it, too."

"Actually, his suite has its own bath. The younger Mr.

Morrell had it installed before he moved in. Unfortunately, that's the only improvement he managed."

At least he wouldn't be in her way. "I could live with those arrangements."

Ella wrung her hands several times before saying, "Then the job is yours if you want it."

Selene decided this was almost too easy. "Wouldn't you like to see my portfolio first? Or at the very least, let me prepare some kind of estimate for my services?"

"That's not necessary. I promise, you'll be paid much more than you would normally receive for this type of work. I'll have all the details outlined in a simple contract that Mr. Morrell drew up himself."

"What about consulting with him first?"

"He's left the hiring up to me. He trusts my judgment, and my judgment tells me you'll do a fine job."

Could she really afford to decide something so important on the spot? A better question—could she afford *not* to accept since she was armed with an interior design degree that she'd never really utilized and a very limited résumé? If she turned down the offer, she might have to search long and hard for another opportunity, especially one that would allow her the freedom to take a project with so much potential and see it to fruition. "Pending the contract is in order, I'll take the job."

Ella looked very pleased. "Wonderful. When can you move in?"

"Right now if I need to. I'm staying at the local inn. I will have to go back there and get my things." Very few things. Most of what Selene had owned she'd left behind, except for the harsh memories of a doomed marriage.

"Today would be wonderful." Ella started toward the door. "I'll show you the contract first, and while you're in town, I'll see if I can arrange a time for you to meet him."

Him, as in Mr. Morrell, Selene decided. "I'm looking forward to it." If for no other reason aside from curiosity.

"One thing you need to know about Adrien," Ella said once they reentered the hallway. "He's a hard case. I've known him for many years, and the best way to handle him is to stand your ground."

Considering Ella's cautions, Selene wondered if she'd already made a colossal error in judgment. "I'll remember that."

On the drive back to the inn, Selene entertained more than a few second thoughts even though she'd found the agreement satisfactory and the pay much more than generous. She should have questioned the woman more thoroughly, particularly about the mysterious owner. Yet the opportunity had practically fallen into her lap at a time when she'd been uncertain over her future. Sheer serendipity.

Besides, the man was probably a middle-aged codger, as peculiar as his grandfather, set in his ways and, she suspected, cranky. She could handle cranky. She could handle anything as long as she could be her own person, make her own decisions, at least when it came to her private life.

Yes, she would deal with Adrien Morrell, through whatever means necessary, be it killing him with kindness or hanging tough. Better still, she would ignore him altogether.

"Who the hell is she, Ella?"

Adrien immediately noted the surprise in his longtime companion's near black eyes, followed by a flicker of guilt before she said, "You've seen her?"

Yes, he'd seen her. He'd watched her from the window as she'd left her car. Saw her brief hesitation. Witnessed her wariness. He'd noticed the way her golden blond hair, bound at her neck, spiraled down her back in soft curls. Noticed her slender throat, her flawless pale skin, the length of her legs and the curve of her hips. From the shadows near the stairs, he'd also observed her walking the corridor, and imagined more than only watching her. A reaction he didn't welcome but hadn't been able to stop.

Adrien leaned forward and rolled a pen back and forth over the desk's surface. "What does she want?"

"A job."

He tossed the pen aside. "I assume you told her she was in the wrong place."

"No, I did not." Ella stepped forward from the door and displayed her usual toughness. "Her name is Selene Winston, and I've hired her to oversee the restoration."

A sharp prick of seething anger threatened Adrien's tenuous self-control. "I didn't give you permission to hire anyone."

Ella planted her palms on the desk and leaned into them. "Someone needs to go forward with the plans before this house falls down around our heads."

Damn her interference. "That's my decision, not yours."

"That's the problem, *shâ*. You're making no decisions. That's why we need someone to get this place into shape so you can put it on the market and leave."

Right now he didn't care to leave. The house had become his haven, his own private hell. "How did you find her?"

"I put an ad in the St. Edwards newspaper and she answered it. She's the *only* one who answered it. And you're the one who told me you wanted someone who would give the house personal attention. Otherwise, I could have hired a firm from Baton Rouge months ago."

Adrien didn't like the way Ella's gaze suddenly faltered. "Where is she from?"

"Georgia. She's a divorcée. From the looks of her car and clothes, I suspect she has money, or did at one time. But for some reason she's decided to settle in St. Edwards. As long as she's a hard worker, I don't really care how she got here."

Adrien cared. He had no use for a woman who'd probably never had her diamond-bedecked hands dirty in her whole damn life. "How much experience does she have?"

She shrugged. "Why don't you ask her since you're the all-knowing, all-seeing entrepreneur?"

If Ella were anyone else, he'd fire her. "I really don't give a damn because I have no intention of letting her stay."

"You don't give a damn about anything, Adrien." She straightened and sighed. "It's been well over a year now. You have to go on with your life."

A life filled with remorse. A life that had become static, by his own hand. And he liked it that way. "Tell her she's not needed here." Or wanted.

Ella scowled. "Oh, she's needed here, all right. And she's staying, or I'll go with her."

More empty threats, Adrien decided. Nothing he hadn't witnessed before from his surrogate mother. Ella wasn't going anywhere because she had no desire to leave him alone. In order to keep the peace, at least externally if not internally, he'd humor her for now. "Fine. Do what you will. Just make sure she stays out of my way."

"Maybe you should tell her yourself. She's agreed to live here until the house is finished. I put her in the room next to yours." With that, Ella spun around without giving him a glance and headed out the door.

Adrien streaked both hands down his face and leaned back in his chair. He didn't need any of this. Didn't need this Winston woman anywhere near him. Even if she was beautiful. Even if he'd been numb for months now and when he'd seen her, he'd begun to come alive, at least in a carnal sense.

He'd be damned if he'd bed some Georgia debutante,

and he had every intention of persuading her to leave. He wasn't exactly sure how he would manage it, but he would. He definitely would.

Selene had been granted a delay in the official meeting, at least for the time being. According to Ella, the plantation's owner hadn't requested an audience, nor had he joined them for dinner. She hadn't run into him on her way to retire for the night, but earlier she had heard him passing through the corridor outside the bedroom, followed by a closing door. The sound of creaking floorboards, as if he'd been pacing, continued for a time before ceasing a few moments ago. Now if only she could get some sleep.

But sleep seemed as elusive as her employer. The fans only served to stir the warm air, and the open windows provided little relief. She'd tossed and turned so much that her thin white gown was practically wrapped around her neck. And although she'd taken a bath before turning in, at this rate she would probably need another. She couldn't imagine how people survived before the advent of air-conditioning. But then they couldn't miss what they'd never had.

What Selene really needed at the moment was some fresh air to provide some temporary comfort. On that thought, she pushed out of the bed, opened the French doors and stepped barefoot onto the veranda, hoping she didn't encounter any splinters jutting up from the wooden decking as she moved to the edge of the balcony. With her hands braced on the black railing, she turned her gaze to the three-quarter moon hanging overhead and the host of stars scattered across the midnight sky.

The temperature had mercifully dropped to a more tolerable level, the gentle wind she'd been seeking flowing over her damp body and ruffling her unruly hair. The bayou's summer sounds surrounded her—chirping locusts and bellowing bullfrogs. She inclined her head and listened for the rush of the Mississippi that knit through the terrain not far away. She only heard the rustle of brush from below. No doubt, the swamps were full of nasty creatures. Probably a few bobcats and alligators with large, treacherous teeth waiting to snap up unsuspecting wildlife. Definitely snakes slithering about, coiled and ready to strike. Maybe even a wolf foraging the forest, searching for prey.

A brief image flashed in her mind—another mental photo shoot of someone watching her—followed by a low, rugged male voice saying, "Too hot to sleep?"

Two

Selene spun to her right to find a dark figure seated in a wicker settee at the end of the veranda a few feet away. She released a ragged breath, one hand resting on her chest above the gown's scooped neck, the other gripping the rail tighter for support. "You startled me."

"Obviously." His tone dripped with sarcasm.

Wonderful. A midnight encounter with a jerk. She was so looking forward to this. "I take it you're Mr. Morrell."

"Correct."

That relieved Selene somewhat, even if his attitude needed adjusting. At least he was a real man, not some ghostly apparition.

What now? She could bid him good-night and return to her room. Or she could get the official introduction out of the way then go back to bed. With that in mind, she shored up her courage and moved closer, the moonlight providing enough illumination for her to make out a few details.

Details such as he couldn't be much beyond his mid-thirties and not the curmudgeon she'd envisioned.

His slightly wavy dark hair fell below his chin and his lips formed a line as hard and unyielding as his jaw that was covered in evening whiskers. Then her gaze came to rest on his eyes. She suspected the same eyes that had flashed in her mind upon her arrival. Unearthly blue, predatory eyes.

She could also see he wasn't wearing a shirt, while she was wearing a cotton gown that provided little cover. Not necessarily the proper attire for her first encounter with her boss, but she might as well get it over with.

Selene finally gathered enough wherewithal to step forward and offer her hand along with a forced smile. "I'm your new employee, Selene Winston."

"I know who you are." His gaze tracked down her body slowly in a blatant size-up before he centered it on her extended hand. After a slight hesitation, he took her palm into his grasp and curled his fingers around hers. Selene reeled from the bolt of sensation, the abject pain emanating from him. A deep, wounding pain.

She quickly dropped her hand and took a step back, as if she'd suffered an electrical shock. In reality, she had. She'd lived with the "gift" for as long as she could remember, keeping it concealed from the world. Well-bred Southern girls didn't read minds; they read the society page. But in all her years, never before had she been empathetic. She'd been able to discern others thoughts through imagery and occasionally words, but she'd never been able to channel feelings. Until him.

"It's nice to meet you," she murmured once she again had control over her voice.

He didn't return the greeting, yet he did continue to stare at her, making her want to twitch where she stood.

Making her want to run from him even though she felt oddly drawn to him. Drawn to his aura. His pain.

She struggled for something casual to say despite the uncomfortable situation. "I'd appreciate your input on how you want the restorations handled. Not right now, of course, since I need something to write with. Maybe tomorrow. Or the next day, if you prefer." Heaven help her, she was rambling like an idiot.

He failed to respond for a few moments until he finally said, "Only one thing you need to know. I expect perfection."

Selene knew all about perfection. She'd lived the perfect life with the perfect family. Had gone to perfect schools and had married the perfect man. The perfect lying bastard, she corrected. "I'll do my best to please you."

He laced his hands atop his bare belly. "That remains to be seen. I'm not easy to please."

That certainly didn't surprise Selene considering Ella's assessment that Adrien Morrell was a "hard case." She would have to concur. And after her reaction to him when they'd touched, she sensed that perhaps he had his reasons. "Do you have any particular preferences?"

He inclined his head and surveyed her face from forehead to chin, settling his gaze on her mouth. "In reference to what?"

Another image filtered into her mind, regardless of her attempts to stop it. She only caught a glimpse of his thoughts, but enough to realize those thoughts involved questionable considerations involving naked bodies. *Her* naked body.

Selene couldn't fathom why her well-honed ability to block this kind of thing failed her now. Couldn't understand why he would be fantasizing about her, a woman he'd just met. More disturbing, she couldn't comprehend why that excited her.

"I'm referring to how you would like the restoration handled," she said once the images dissolved.

He shifted slightly in the chair. "I prefer not to be involved at all. Unless you have no idea what you're doing."

That made her bristle, her defenses on high alert. "Any reason why you believe I wouldn't know what I'm doing?"

"You've given me no evidence to believe that you do."

How was she going to answer? Easy. By telling only a partial truth. "I have an interior-design degree. I've also supervised staffs and redecorated my own house in the past. I've even refinished furniture with my own two hands."

"Was that before or after your tennis game with the ladies down at the club?"

She resented his condescending tone. Resented even more that he was right about her former life. "Actually, I believe that was the day I had tea with the Daughters of the Confederacy," she said in her sweetest drawl. "Right before I went to my lessons on how to be genteel and polite even when confronted by ill-mannered jackasses. Those lessons seem to be escaping me now."

He looked as if he might actually smile, but it didn't quite form. "Are you calling me a jackass, Ms. Winston?"

If the moniker fits. She laid a dramatic hand above her breast. "Why, no, Mr. Morrell. That would be totally improper."

Again he raked his gaze down her body and back up again. Slowly. "Nothing wrong with impropriety now and then, Selene."

And no doubt he had that impropriety market cornered. He'd been brazen enough to call her by her given name. Bold enough to fantasize about her. And he hadn't even bothered to stand...until that moment.

He came to his feet slowly and, as she'd guessed, he was

an inch or two over six feet. His chest was lean, well defined and dusted with a layer of dark hair, his flat abdomen sporting a sequence of ridges above the waistband of his black slacks. His proximity alone jumbled her mind, hindered her breathing, as did his scent. A subtle clean scent that seemed perfectly in sync with the summer night, as if he were an integral part of the atmosphere. Mystifying, intoxicating, forbidden.

If he'd meant to intimidate her, it was working. But Selene wasn't going to let that happen. Not anymore. Not by any man. Especially not a man like him, even if he was absolutely awe-inspiring—in a threatening kind of way.

But instead of backing up, she turned her attention to a pair of dark vines circling his solid bicep, a grouping of letters centered in the middle that spelled out the word *Imperium*. "Interesting tattoo. My Latin's a little rusty. What does it mean?"

She lifted her eyes to find his gaze boring into her. "Absolute power."

Both his declaration and his overwhelming presence paralyzed her, even though she knew what he was about to do. The way he studied her mouth again gave her the first indication. His musings that broke through her mental haze served as confirmation. If she didn't leave now, he was going to kiss her. And she might actually let him.

Forcing herself back into reality, Selene folded her arms tightly around herself, as if that might offer some protection, and stepped back to regain her resolve. "I don't believe power is absolute, Mr. Morrell."

With the last of her shredding strength, Selene turned away from him and headed back to the safety of the bedroom. But she'd only managed a few steps before he said, "Some power is absolute, Selene. And you know it."

She didn't dare face him again, or respond at all. Doing

so would only prove to him that he did possess a certain power—over her.

She returned to the room, closing the doors behind her. Closing him out. But she couldn't drive him from her thoughts, nor could she rid herself of the persistent heat that had little to do with the elements.

She climbed into bed and tried to clear her mind. Tried to sleep. Tried to think about anything but him. But as she drifted off, Adrien Morrell was the last thing she thought about. The last thing she saw.

The minute Selene stepped from the bathroom into the hallway the following morning, she knew he had been nearby. She'd immediately caught the scent of his cologne, but more importantly, she sensed his presence. An intangible feeling that totally consumed her. She wondered if he'd been standing at the door or if he'd simply just passed through the corridor. Whatever the case might be, he wasn't anywhere in sight now. That should please her, but in a way, she was disappointed—only because she wanted to get a look at him in the daylight. A good, long look.

Glancing to her right, she intended to check to see if his bedroom door was open. Instead, she made contact with the devilish statue, its vicious features causing her to physically jump. Demon Giles would definitely have to go somewhere else. Anywhere else. If she thought she could actually haul him up and carry him out, she would deposit him in the nearby swamp.

Selene returned to her bedroom, slipped out of her robe and into a pair of white linen slacks and a coral knit sleeveless top. At least her summer apparel provided a respite from the heat that had already begun to creep into the house.

Selene headed down the spiral staircase at a fast clip, relieved to be out of the dark corridor and into the light, surrounded by cherubs. As she made her way across the rotunda toward the kitchen, she paused at a painting hanging on the wall of a young woman with bright green eyes and raven-black hair swept up from her slender, pale neck, her hands folded primly in her lap. Considering the lady's clothing—a soft white, long lace dress with a full skirt—Selene would guess that she'd probably resided at the plantation many years before. But when she studied the inscription on the brass plate anchored to the bottom of the frame, a series of chills raced up her spine as well as a sense of foreboding.

Grace— She sleeps with the angels.

Maybe this was a key to one of the tragedies Ella had spoken about the previous day. Maybe this beautiful young woman had died before her youth was spent, and perhaps even in this house. As disconcerting as that thought was, Selene wanted to know more about the plantation's past, if for no other reason than to satisfy her own curiosity. Who better to ask than the owner's right-hand woman?

As she entered the kitchen, Selene found Ella at the ancient white stove scrambling eggs and humming a cheerful song.

"Good morning," Selene said as she pulled back a chair and took a seat at the weathered pine table.

Ella regarded her over one shoulder while she continued to cook. "Good morning to you, too. Did you sleep well?"

"Fairly well. It's going to take me a while to get used to the surroundings." To get used to the idea that Adrien Morrell resided right next door. She'd intermittently heard the sounds of his footsteps throughout the night, as if he'd been restless. But then so had she. She still was.

Ella turned from the stove, balancing a full plate in one hand and a cup of coffee in the other. She crossed the small space and slid the fare in front of Selene. "Enjoy."

Selene resisted wrinkling her nose. She didn't care for

eggs or bacon. Toast she could do, and coffee. Definitely coffee. "It looks good, but I'm never very hungry in the morning. I also want to get an early start today."

Ella returned to the table with her own cup of coffee and took the chair across from Selene. "If you stay around for a while, you might be able to meet Mr. Morrell when he comes down for breakfast."

"I've already met him." Selene waited for Ella's apparent surprise to subside before she added, "Last night, on the veranda outside our rooms."

Ella slid a fingertip around the rim of her own cup. "How did that go?"

It had gone places Selene had never expected. "Not too badly. He wanted to know about my work experience, and I got the impression he doesn't want to be bothered with the details of the restoration."

Ella sighed. "He wants to be left alone."

Selene had sensed that about him last night, even in light of his fantasies about her. "What exactly does he do for a living?"

"He's an entrepreneur. He turned his inheritance into a small fortune through various ventures, mainly buying faltering businesses, restoring them and selling them for a large profit. He's very good at what he does, or he was until…" Ella's gaze drifted away with her words.

"Until what?" Selene asked.

"Until he decided to take a break from it all."

Again, Selene wanted to know more about Adrien, to ask more questions. But she sensed Ella wasn't up to answering, which called for a subject change. "If you can point me to a phone, I'll contact a few prospective contractors and set up appointments."

Ella took a quick sip of her coffee. "You'll have to find someone from Baton Rouge since you won't find anyone locally, at least not anyone who's willing to come out here. The townspeople are a superstitious lot. They believe the place is cursed."

Ella had unknowingly provided Selene with a good opening. "That portrait near the staircase. Is that woman somehow involved in the tragedies?"

"I'm not really sure," Ella said. "I assume she probably is, but I don't know any details about her."

Selene had always embraced the past, and she truly believed the woman named Grace had an interesting one at that.

She took another quick drink of coffee, pushed back from the table and stood. "I'm going to go into town and pay a personal visit to a few of the business owners. Maybe someone can suggest a local contractor who isn't superstitious."

"Good luck." Ella nodded toward Selene's untouched food. "You should eat something first, put on a few pounds so you don't make me look quite so portly."

"You're fine just the way you are. And I'm in a hurry to get this restoration underway." In a hurry to get away because she sensed Adrien's imminent arrival as surely as if she'd heard his approaching footsteps, which she hadn't. Any minute now, he could walk into the kitchen and throw her off balance. Better to head into town before that happened. Before she had to look at him again, this time in the daylight where all her fascination and preoccupation with her boss would be bared like a flashing billboard. Because she was fascinated by him, completely intrigued. He had his share of secrets, that much she knew, and most she would probably never know.

Yet she also knew those secrets had brought on his pain, and she had always been a sucker for lost souls. She'd manned a couple of hotlines on a volunteer basis, had championed several causes. She'd also learned that some lost people didn't care to be found. She suspected that Adrien Morrell had no desire to be saved from his solitude. For that reason alone, she vowed to pay no heed to him, as long as he stayed out of her head.

Alone in his office, Adrien stood at the window and watched Selene Winston drive away. Curiosity sent him immediately to her room, to see if she had left for good. In his experience, everyone eventually left. Not so in this case, at least not yet.

The white gown she'd been wearing on the veranda last night was draped over the bed's footboard. The sheer fabric had revealed only a few details, but enough details to set him on edge and keep him there. Striding across the room, he passed his palm over the gown that was as soft as her skin. He knew that much, even though he hadn't touched her. Yet. But he would.

Last night, he'd warred with what was wise and what he wanted. Many considered him predatory, territorial in both business and in pleasure. Until recently, he'd lived for the thrill of the chase, the rewards of capture. Selene Winston had resurrected that desire. Though he'd made a solid effort to ignore his baser urges, he was still a man. A man on a mission.

He planned to draw her into his world with a slow and carefully crafted seduction, guiding her into the darkness he'd created. She might be reluctant at first, but eventually she would come without reservation. Willingly. Openly.

She would provide a respite from his remorse, a means to temporarily forget what he hadn't done. More importantly, what he *had* done…to Chloe.

Fifteen minutes later, Selene drove into St. Edwards and pulled her sedan in front of Abby's Antiques, a place she had visited several times. The shop was situated along a row of small businesses that lined the single downtown street, an ancient red brick church serving as the town's cornerstone. After only a moment's hesitation, she left the car and entered the glass door, the subtle chime announcing her arrival.

The proprietor, Abby Reynolds, a fortysomething tiny woman with bobbed auburn hair and kind hazel eyes, looked up from behind the counter positioned at the back of the store and greeted Selene with a smile. "Hello, Ms. Winston. I thought you'd left town."

"As it turns out, I'm going to be here awhile." Selene skirted the helter-skelter antiques as she traveled down the narrow aisle, basking in the blessedly cool air flowing over her. If only she could bottle some to take back to the plantation.

When Selene reached the counter, Abby pushed her black glasses up onto her head and set aside the book she'd been reading. "You've decided to stay?"

"Yes, thanks to you. Remember that ad you showed me? As it turns out, it's a plantation west of town, and I've been hired to oversee a complete restoration."

"Maison de Minuit." Selene immediately noticed the wariness in Abby's tone and the stiffness of her small frame. "That should be challenging."

"Yes it will be, and that's why I'm here." Selene set her purse on the counter and folded her hands next to it. "Do you happen to know a local contractor who'd be willing to take it on?"

The woman shook her head. "You won't find anyone here who'll go out there."

Exactly what Ella had told Selene earlier. "What is it about the place that has everyone avoiding it like the plague?"

"Well, there's the matter of the lovers who supposedly

died there, and the voodoo woman who lived there after that. And the somewhat insane Giles Morrell who fortunately wasn't there very long. Take your pick."

Selene wondered if Grace happened to be one of those lovers. "Do you know any details? Names, that sort of thing? I'd like to know a little bit about the plantation's history."

Abby shrugged. "I've only been in town a couple of years. When I have heard people speak about the place, it's been brief, as if they're afraid to talk about it. And there's also the woman who mysteriously disappeared about a year ago."

"What woman?" Selene couldn't mask her surprise or uneasiness.

"Supposedly Adrien Morrell was holed up with her for over a year," Abby said. "Ralph Allen works for a delivery service and used to make runs out there every week or so to deliver packages. He says he saw her looking out an upstairs window a couple of times."

Surely Adrien didn't have an unidentified woman locked up in the mysterious bedroom. A totally ludicrous thought, Selene decided. Still... "But as far as anyone knows, she left?"

"The deliveries stopped suddenly, and no one's seen her since. Except Ralph swears he passed a coroner's car coming from that direction one morning."

Selene swallowed hard. "She died?"

Abby showed her discomfort by shifting her weight from one hip to the other. "There isn't any real proof of that. No death notice or anything. But Mr. Morrell has enough money to pay for silence, so I guess anything's possible. If he wanted her dead, he could arrange for it, even if he didn't do it himself."

Selene wasn't sure she wanted to explore those possibilities, though she didn't really view Adrien as a murderer. But what did she really know about him? Not much, other than he was a physically attractive, powerful man. "Maybe she just left on her own accord."

"Maybe she was a ghost." Abby attempted a reassuring smile. "You know how it is with gossip, Selene. People are like coon hounds with a rawhide bone. They chew on it for a while, then bury it for a time, but they always bring it out, along with more dirt."

Selene wanted to believe that that's all it was—idle gossip from the depths of idle minds. Rumor or not, she was still uneasy. "Do you know anyone who knows about the plantation's previous owners? Maybe a historian of some kind?"

"Unfortunately, the town doesn't have a library, otherwise I'd point you in that direction. You could try the courthouse, but I don't know how far back their records go. They don't even have a computerized system yet. And they lost quite a bit during a flood in the 1920s."

That sounded like a surefire dead end to Selene. "I suppose it wouldn't hurt to try that."

"Good luck," Abby said. "In the meantime, I can ask around and let you know if I find someone who knows the history."

"That would be wonderful." Selene rummaged through her purse, withdrew a pen and paper, jotted down her number, then handed it to Abby. "This is my cell phone. You can call me anytime."

Abby reached beneath the counter, took out a notepad and began to write. "I'm going to give you the address of a friend of mine, Linda Adams. She's in Baton Rouge and she specializes in antique restoration." She tore off the page and slid it in front of Selene. "She can help you with fabric selection and anything you need done with the furnishings. Her husband's a contractor and he's worked on several historical homes in the area, so he might be willing to help you out."

Selene took the paper and tucked it into the side pocket of her bag. "Thanks so much. I'll pay her a visit today."

After giving her thanks and a goodbye to Abby, Selene slid into her car for the trip to Baton Rouge. But before she could pull out into the street, a name jumped into her mind, as clear as the sound of the church's bell now tolling in the town square. The name meant nothing to her at all, but the voice that spoke it did.

Adrien Morrell's voice.

"Who's Chloe?" Following the query, Selene watched her dinner companion's expression herald first shock, then caution.

"Where did you hear that name?" Ella asked.

"In town." She didn't dare tell her exactly where the name had originated—in her mind.

Ella sent her a suspicious glance before pushing the pile of peas around on her plate. "That's not possible. No one in town knows about her."

"They believe a woman named Chloe was here for a while with Mr. Morrell, and then she was gone. Rumor has it she died."

Ella dropped her fork, pushed her plate aside and folded her hands tightly before her on the table. "First, you can't always believe what you hear, Selene. Second, I don't know who told you about her, but if I were you, I'd drop it. Now."

Selene couldn't ignore Ella's adamant tone, or the hint of anger. She worried that if she pushed too hard, Ella might push back. Or worse, dismiss her immediately regardless of the contract. "I drove into Baton Rouge today and found a woman who's going to help me restore the furniture. Her husband has agreed to come by and give us an estimate on repairs. But he's busy until next week."

Ella thankfully smiled. "You definitely accomplished quite a bit today."

"I also went by the courthouse," Selene added. "The woman told me it would take several days for her to locate any plans, and that's if they actually have any. Do you think I might find some here?"

Ella shrugged. "I'm sure Adrien probably has a set, but you'll have to ask him."

Not something Selene wanted to do, at least not tonight. "Is there some kind of attic where I might find old documents, maybe original abstracts?"

Ella picked up both hers and Selene's plates, then stood. "Yes, there's an attic. You'll find the door at the end of the hallway past Adrien's office. Feel free to explore it." The look Ella sent her said, "If you dare."

"Think I'll check it out in the next few days." In the daylight, Selene decided, because she definitely didn't want to traipse around in a dusty attic in the dark, in case she should come across the stuff scary legends were made of, including an idiot. That thought almost made her laugh. Almost.

Selene pushed back from the table and stood. "Let me do the dishes."

Ella waved a hand in dismissal. "I'll do them, dear."

"I insist," Selene said as she began to gather the serving bowls. "I could use something to do while I think."

"In case you haven't noticed, we don't have a dishwasher."

Selene had noticed, and that would be the first appliance on the purchase list. "I have no problem using my own two hands."

Ella sent her a cynical smile. "Have you ever washed dishes before, dear?"

"As a matter of fact, I have." Much to her mother's horror.

"Then I'll gratefully take you up on your offer. I need to speak with Adrien before I retire, anyway."

Most likely reporting to him about the new employee, Selene decided. But that didn't really matter. So far, she had done nothing wrong other than bring up the name Chloe. And although she'd decided to steer clear of that topic for now, she suspected Ella knew much more than she was willing to reveal. A mystery that might never be solved, unless Selene made a conscious—or subconscious—effort to solve it.

No. She wouldn't invade someone's mind to gain information. She'd done that before, only to suffer for it. If she discovered anything at all, it would have to come from someone verbally volunteering the information, not by her intruding into an unsuspecting mind. She highly doubted Adrien Morrell would serve as that volunteer, even though she instinctively knew he held the key. But then again, she might not want to know.

Adrien didn't bother to look up from the newspaper, even when Ella slid the covered plate and utensils in front of him. "If it's cold, don't blame me. You should come to dinner like a normal person."

He sent a disinterested glance at the food before finally bringing his attention to Ella. "I'm sure it's fine."

Ella remained in the same spot, obviously in the mood for a little chat. "Don't you want to know what our new houseguest has been doing?"

He knew exactly what she'd been doing—keeping him in sexual high gear, and she didn't even realize it. Yet. He went back to the paper, hoping Ella might take the hint and leave. "I've told you, I'm not interested in her plans." But he was definitely interested in her.

"She's been asking about the house's history," Ella continued despite his comment. "I thought you might like to help her out with that."

Adrien only wanted to help her out with one thing, and it had nothing to do with the past. He was much more interested in the immediate future. After folding the paper in precise creases, he set it aside. "What do you suggest?"

"First, she needs a set of blueprints," she said.

He opened a drawer, withdrew a cardboard tube and offered it to her. "Here."

Ella waved his offer of the plans. "You give them to her. It wouldn't kill you to be nice to her."

If Ella only knew how badly he wanted to be *nice* to Selene, she'd probably rescind the suggestion. "I'll think about it. But right now, I have some work to do. Anything else that needs my attention?"

"Yes, *shâ*. Your manners."

She spun around and headed out the door before Adrien could even offer a parting good-night. He wasn't expecting to have a good night. He'd rarely had one for almost two years now. Sleep had been as elusive as peace over the past months, and last night had been no exception. It hadn't helped that he'd encountered a woman who had shattered all his expectations. A woman who'd started a slow burn that had begun to heat up at a rapid pace.

Maybe Selene would like to spend a little time with him tonight. If she wanted to explore some history, he could accommodate her. He would willingly take her on a different kind of exploration, if she gave him some kind of sign she welcomed his attention. He had no cause to think she might, at least not now.

But he wouldn't let that deter him. He would have never gotten anywhere in business if he'd avoided challenges. Now he had to convince Selene Winston she had nothing to fear from him, as long as she never learned the truth.

Three

When Selene crossed through the "angel arena" on the way to her room, an eerie feeling slowed her steps on her ascent up the spiral staircase. As she turned the corner into the dark corridor, her heart immediately jumped into her throat. A few feet away, Adrien stood in the hallway, dressed in a steel-gray shirt and black slacks, one shoulder leaned against the wall, hands firmly planted in his pockets. He was as stone-still as the statue behind him, although he had much more physical appeal.

Selene planned to send him a polite greeting and good-night before she retired to her room. But before she could even utter a word, he said, "Going to bed already?"

His voice was low and provocative, but then so was he. A sullen stranger set in shadows. The light was muted, but at least now she could fully appreciate the details of a face that could have been sculpted by the angels keeping vigil nearby. No horrid disfigurement.

No mask of death. No real innocence, either, especially when it came to his eyes. Those deadly cut-glass blue eyes that he kept trained on her while she simply stood there as if in a trance.

Again Selene hugged her arms to her middle and finally snapped out of her stupor. "I've had a busy day," she said. "I'm tired."

He pushed off the wall but kept a safe distance. "Too tired for a little adventure?"

The question shook Selene's waning calm so strongly she couldn't speak for a few moments. "What kind of adventure?"

He took a slow step toward her. "Ella told me you're interested in the history of this house. I have something that might satisfy you."

His emphasis on *satisfy* shook her up even more. "What exactly would that be?"

"I could tell you, but I'd prefer to show you."

Selene checked her watch, more out of nervousness than true concern with the time. Although it was barely past nine, she said, "It is getting late."

"I'll make it worth your while."

He'd lowered his voice a notch and Selene responded with a slight shiver. A pleasant one that was both unexpected and inadvisable. "Where exactly would we be going for this adventure?"

He nodded toward the opposite end of the corridor. "To my office."

An office seemed relatively safe, but could she really be safe around him? She had two options—to trust him or use her gift to sift through his thoughts. She opened her mind briefly, but came up with nothing. No visions of him holding her hostage or doing her bodily harm. At least not yet.

"Lead the way." The words spilled out of her mouth

without any further consideration. If she really intended to work for him, she had to give him some of her trust, unless he proved he didn't deserve it. And hopefully not after it was too late for her to turn back.

She followed him down the hall, past the stairway and into the wing Ella had described to her during the initial tour, a place she had yet to explore. They passed by the closed door leading to the nursery, Selene presumed. When they reached another door adjacent to that, Adrien opened it and stepped aside for her to enter.

The large office was thoroughly modern, from the solid oak desk lit by a lone lamp to the computer sitting on a counter in the corner. Several binders were stacked neatly in an in-box and a silver canister housed various pens. Everything in its place and not at all what Selene had expected. But at least the room was sufficiently cool. In fact, it was cooler than most of the house, thanks to that modern convenience known as a window unit. Might have been nice if someone had bothered to install them everywhere.

When she heard the door close behind her, Selene fought the urge to spin around and display some serious panic. For all intents and purposes, she was trapped. He could do with her what he wanted and she doubted Ella would hear a single cry of distress.

Still, she wasn't getting any strange vibes or sense of looming disaster. When she faced him, she did get the full effect of Adrien's slight smile. The first she'd witnessed so far. "What do you want to show me?"

He slid his hands into his pockets again and looked much more relaxed than she felt. "A journal."

Selene had learned nothing was of more value in recreating the past than personal writings. "Where is it?" she asked, her tone revealing her enthusiasm over the discovery.

Adrien crossed the room to his right, opened a door and flipped on a light. "Up here."

Selene moved closer to see a dimly lit, narrow staircase and made a mental note to have someone replace all the low-wattage bulbs in the house as soon as possible. She took a mental step back when she realized she would have to accompany her employer into a remote area. "It looks like you might find a bat or two up there." She'd said it with humor to mask her wariness.

He hinted at another smile. "No bats, but maybe a few spiders."

"Lovely."

He studied her for a moment. "Are you afraid of spiders, Selene?"

Insects had never been her best friends, but she wasn't exactly arachnophobic. "No. As long as they keep their distance."

"Are you afraid of me?"

A very good question, one that Selene needed to seriously ponder. "Any reason why I should be?"

"Not at all."

He sounded convincing to Selene, but could she really believe him? She could usually rely on her instincts, though, and they were telling her he had no plans to injure her. As far as any other plans went—questionable plans—she supposed she would have to take her chances and keep a firm grip on self-control.

She made a sweeping gesture toward the staircase. "After you."

He took the first step and when she hung back, he shifted slightly and offered his hand. "I'll make sure you don't fall."

Selene wasn't all that concerned with falling. Years of ballet lessons had cured her of any serious clumsiness. But she was concerned about touching him again. Concerned that she might experience another blow to her senses. Yet instead of insisting on managing without his help, she reached out and accepted his offered hand. This time, the contact sent a rush of heat coursing through her body, as if she were being warmed from the inside out. The sensation was overwhelming and as they started to ascend the stairs, it only grew more intense. He glanced back at her now and then with eyes as blue as the ceiling in the rotunda. By the time they reached the top, Selene was both winded and very, very warm, even when he released his grasp on her.

The landing opened into another room, this one smaller with a narrow shelf housing volumes of aged books. In the corner sat a mahogany pedestal desk, and a lone straight-backed chair covered in red satin. The area was dusty, the ceiling draped with a few cobwebs, but other than that, it didn't look at all menacing. At least where bats and bugs were concerned.

"At one time this was the *garçonnière*," Adrien said as he remained at her side. "The original bachelor's quarters, probably used by a previous owner."

But obviously not used by Adrien, Selene thought. "Your grandfather?"

He forked a hand through his hair. "No. Giles wasn't one to stay in the same place for very long. He had a solid case of wanderlust. I inherited that from him."

She sent him a smile. "You're inclined to travel, I take it."

"Not in a while." He strolled to the bookshelves then faced her again. "I've been all over the world. Europe. Africa. Central America. Mostly off the beaten path. Spain is one of my favorite spots."

She walked to the desk and leaned against it. "Don't tell me. You've run with the bulls in Pamplona."

"Actually, no. I would be more inclined to root for the bulls since I believe that animals sometimes have more merit than humans."

A point in his favor, Selene decided. "So you're a thrill seeker as long as it doesn't involve cruelty to animals."

"At one time, yes."

He looked and sounded regretful, and that only served to spur Selene's interest. "I've been to Europe several times," she said to break the brief span of uncomfortable silence. "Mostly London. The usual tourist spots."

He rested one elbow on the edge of the shelf. "Ever done any cliff diving in Mexico?"

She laughed. "I'm not fond of heights."

"Ever stood on a deserted beach, naked, and watched the sun come up?"

Only in her wildest dreams. "I'm afraid not."

"You should experience it at some point in time."

Little did he know, he'd taken her there through his recollections, images that were too strong to bar from her mind. She experienced the salty breeze blowing over her bare skin and the sun on her face, smelled the scents of the sea, felt his palms forming to her waist, curving over her abdomen and lower....

Forcing herself out of his fantasy, she turned her attention to the shelves to avoid his steady gaze. "I've often wondered what it would have been like to live years ago, when times were less complex and modern conveniences were nonexistent."

"I've been in places where you had to rely solely on nature," he said. "It's a rush."

Selene decided his deep, steady voice was a rush. "I'm too old and set in my ways to rough it too much."

He inclined his head and narrowed his eyes to assess her. "You're what, maybe late twenties?"

"Thirty-two. And you?"

"Thirty-five. How old were you when you married?"

Obviously he knew much more about her than she knew about him. "Twenty-four. I've been divorced for a year."

He paced the room's perimeter, glancing at her now and then, as if he were some wild, agitated creature of the night assessing his quarry. "Seven years, just in time for that proverbial itch."

"You could definitely say that."

He stopped and leaned back against the shelves a few feet away from her. "Did that itch include both of you?"

As much as she wanted to know Adrien better, she was growing increasingly uncomfortable with the conversation. Drudging up her past with Richard always made her ill at ease. "Maybe you could show me the journal now."

"If that's what you want."

He headed straight for her with slow, stalking steps and Selene's gaze immediately tracked to his mouth, the softness of his lips that contrasted with the rigid set of his jaw, the slight cleft in his chin. All too late she realized he'd noticed her interest when he showed some semblance of another smile. Knowing. Sensual.

When he reached the desk, Selene stifled a catch of breath even though he passed by her. She regarded him over her shoulder to see him opening a drawer and withdrawing a small black journal that had seen better days. Olden days, she would guess.

Adrien rounded the desk and offered it to her. "I've marked the place that might interest you."

She took the diary, opened it where a pale pink satin ribbon indicated the spot and noted the date at the top of the page—July 1875. But before she could scan the faded script, Adrien said, "Read it out loud."

She turned her attention from the page to him. "You haven't read it?"

"Yes, I have. But I want to hear your voice."

His voice was so indisputably sensuous, so compelling that Selene couldn't think of one argument. She turned and laid the journal open on the desk while he began pacing the room once more. After clearing her throat, she began to read.

"'This afternoon, I again met Z. at the abandoned share-cropper's cabin near the swamp at his plantation. Should my father discover I am keeping company with his enemy, he would be furious. If he knew what I have done, he would surely kill him.'"

Selene paused and glanced back at Adrien to find him no more than a foot away. "Who wrote this?"

"I don't know. I came across it one day a few months ago."

"I'm wondering if maybe the woman named Grace in the portrait downstairs is the author."

"That's possible," he said. "Keep going."

Selene went back to the journal, driven by her need to know more about the unidentified author's rendezvous. "'I have given freely of my affections to Z., accepted his stolen kisses. He spoke to me about the ways between a man and a woman, and told me things that any proper lady would never consider. Yet I listened, and then I begged him to show me.'"

Again she glanced back at Adrien only to discover he'd moved closer. "I'm feeling a bit like a voyeur."

"I think it's an interesting commentary on the mores of the past," he said. "But if it makes you uncomfortable, hand it to me and I'll read it."

She noted the challenge in his tone, and she intended to answer it. After all, they were both adults, and she highly doubted anything written in this journal would compare to what was featured in modern literature in terms of sexuality. "I'll do it."

After drawing in a deep breath, she turned her attention back to the journal entry. "'In Z.'s arms, I am a wanton. I barely recognize myself. I allowed him to lower my chemise, allowed him to touch my breasts. Never before have I experienced such pleasure. Never before have I been so open or so free. I wanted more. I wanted all that he could give me.'"

Selene's words faltered when a hand came to rest on her shoulder. *Adrien's hand.* As his fingertips idled over her bare arm, she tried to ignore the rhythmic, enticing motion. Tried to disregard the frisson of pleasure brought about by his touch. "Continue," he whispered. "It only gets better."

Good judgment failed Selene and so did her resolve to avoid this very thing. "'He lifted my skirt and slid his hand beneath my drawers. He touched my most secret place, touched me in ways I had never imagined. My body was no longer mine. It belonged to him….'"

Adrien chose that moment to slide his hand down Selene's hip, brushing her pelvis briefly before settling his palm on her lower abdomen. She studied his golden skin against her white slacks, the width of his hand, his blunt fingers. He moved completely against her, his solid chest meeting her back.

She only had enough strength to close the journal and mutter, "That's enough for now." But she didn't push his hand away. Didn't scold him. Didn't move.

"It's not enough."

As if he'd bound her with invisible twine and gave it a tug, she slowly turned to face him. She knew exactly what he planned to do when the image flashed in her mind a split second before he lowered his head.

The minute Adrien's mouth met hers, Selene stepped

into a sensory minefield, bombarded by his subtle, clean scent, the taste of scotch on his lips, the suggestive foray of his tongue against hers. And suddenly it seemed she'd melted into his body, into his soul, experiencing his pleasure as well as her own. Because of this psychic communion, she also knew he needed more from her, wanted more from her.

Still, she had no desire to escape him, no will left to fight. No cause to loosen the grasp she now had on his shoulders even though she'd lost all grip on reality. But the mental as well as the physical connection ended when he stepped back and scrubbed a hand over his jaw.

"My apologies," he said. "I forgot myself for a few minutes."

As far as Selene was concerned, he hadn't forgotten a thing. The kiss had been part of a carefully crafted plan of seduction, and she'd walked right into his trap without a moment's hesitation.

She reached back, picked up the journal from the desk and tapped it against her open palm. "I'm going to read the rest of this later, and we'll forget what just happened."

He backed up a few steps and hid his hands in pockets again. "Go ahead and try to forget it."

I won't....

His thought came to Selene as sharp as a dagger, traveled along the mental passage connecting her mind with his. "We need to maintain a professional relationship."

He brandished his grin like a pirate wielding a sword, cutting her determination to shreds. "A little late for that."

All heaven and hell might break loose if she didn't escape that instant. Self-preservation sent her to the door, clutching the journal to her chest. "I'm going to my room now."

"One more thing, Selene."

The soft sound of her name sliding from his lips acted on her like a potent magnet, drawing her around to face him, where she found him holding out a cardboard tube. "What's that?"

"The plans for the house."

She moved only close enough to take the tube from his grasp. "Thank you."

"And let me set you straight on something. I didn't hire you. Ella did. As far as I'm concerned, you work for her, not me. Which means we don't have a professional relationship. In fact, if I'd had my way, you would already be gone."

Selene was so incredulous she almost couldn't speak. "Is that what this whole thing is all about? You're trying to drive me away?"

"In the beginning, yes. But not now. Not any longer. I've decided I like having you here."

Without responding, Selene turned, sprinted down the narrow steps and kept a fast pace until she reached the safety of her bedroom. But she feared she might never be safe as long as she lived under the same roof with him.

As she readied for bed, her thoughts kept turning to the absolute bliss she'd experienced in his arms. Too many years had passed since a man had touched her that way, or kissed her with such command.

Looking for a distraction, Selene climbed into bed and opened the diary to the place where she'd left off earlier.

We met again today at the cabin although I realized the risk in that. Yet I could not stay away from Z. He kissed me again and again, and I trembled with pleasure. I craved his touch. He then took my hand and placed it against his trousers where I felt his hardness. He said that when he was certain I was ready, he would join his body to mine. I insisted I was ready, I pleaded with him to show me. At first he denied me, but when I opened my arms to him, it was as if I had unleashed something wild in him, my sweet, gentle Z. He tore away his clothes and removed mine before laying me back on the cot to fill my body. I experienced some pain, as he told me I would, but the pain did not compare to the pleasure.

I knew in those moments I was forever his. I knew that no matter what the future held, he would always be mine. But I fear our time might end in terrible ways after today, for as I left the cabin, I saw one of my father's field hands lurking in the swamp, and knew I had been caught. I have no idea what fate awaits me and my lover when my father returns from Savannah tomorrow. I only know that whatever happens, every moment I have spent in Z.'s arms will have been worth it. He is my all. My one true love.

Disappointed to find the journal ended with that passage, Selene closed the diary, turned down the light and tried to sleep. She thought about the mysterious lovers and questioned how a man could have so much power over a woman that she would risk it all to be with him. Perhaps even risk her own life.

No doubt about it, Adrien Morrell had cast his spell over Selene. Now it was up to her to break free, before she, too, found herself caught in the clutches of obsession and allowed him to do anything he pleased.

She was quickly becoming his obsession.

Adrien knew all about obsession. Possession. Once he set a plan in motion, be it business or pleasure, he dove in with dogged determination until he got what he wanted. And he wanted her.

Tonight had been a first step toward his goal. A good step. He'd expected her to resist him a little more, but instead she had responded to his kiss with surprising enthusiasm. Unfortunately, even that minimal contact had set him on fire.

After stripping out of all his clothes, he downed the last bit of scotch, set the glass aside and walked to the double doors leading outside. He parted the curtains to see if Selene had ventured onto the veranda, as she had the other night. He found only an empty balcony to match the emptiness in his soul.

He shut off the lights, stretched out on his back across the bed and ran a slow hand down his abdomen. Knowing Selene was only a few steps away made him harder than he'd been in some time. Had him gritting his teeth and firming his resolve not to go to her. He wouldn't do that until he had an invitation. And he expected to have one, signed, sealed and delivered, very soon.

Right now, he would do whatever he had to do to keep his need for her in check—until the time was right.

He sat motionless at the end of the veranda in the same wicker sofa he'd occupied when Selene had first met him. The full moon cast his imposing frame in bluish light, yet it failed to soften his features, particularly his eyes. Those spellbinding eyes that he kept aimed on her. He looked every bit the stoic king holding court. A dark king.

Totally entranced, Selene maintained her distance a few feet away, watching, waiting. Waiting for him to speak, to move. To say her name.

Like a practiced hypnotist, he called to her simply with his gaze and a slight nod of his head. She effortlessly walked toward him, her mind caught in a fog, her lungs all but absent of air. She noticed immediately the lack of noise—

no rustling breeze, no sounds from the swamp below. Not even the chirp of a cricket. Although she found that odd, she kept moving forward until she stood before him. She also realized he was completely nude—and aroused.

Though he didn't utter a word, she recognized exactly what he wanted. As if bankrupt of free will, she clasped the hem of her gown, pulled it over her head and dropped it onto the ground beside her. Without the least bit of hesitation, she reached out and took his extended hand, allowed him to position her thighs on either side of his thighs. She released a soundless sigh when he lifted her up, then guided himself inside her. The sensations were potent, indescribable. She wanted more, needed more. Needed him to alleviate the dull ache, erase all the years of disappointment. Yet when he failed to move, she knew what he was asking of her. Knew that he waited for her to move first. She began a steady cadence and, in that moment, she became a woman she didn't recognize. An uninhibited woman who strived to please him, as well as herself, as he joined her in reckless abandon.

Still, there was no noise, no sounds of broken breaths, no quiet moans of satisfaction. Only absolute silence. Selene could feel the beat of her heart, the flutter of her pulse, the pressure beginning to build as she hurled toward a climax. Then Adrien stopped moving altogether and buried his face in the cleft of her breasts.

She wanted to ask why he had stopped, but she couldn't speak. She could only lift his head and force him to look at her. Again she saw his utter pain immediately before his face began to blur and fade completely, followed by a flash of white light that blinded her.

Selene forced her eyes open and bolted upright. She wasn't on the veranda, or outside at all. She was in bed.

Frantically she searched the darkened room, only to

discover she was completely alone. She patted her body to find her gown was still intact. Obviously she'd been dreaming. A very detailed dream that had seemed so very, very real.

Then awareness dawned. No, not a dream at all. A fantasy. *His fantasy.*

Selene collapsed back onto the mattress and rolled to her side, taking the spare pillow and slipping it between her knees. Adrien had unwittingly invaded her mind, bringing with him erotic images that she wouldn't soon forget. She couldn't comprehend why she was so open to his thoughts, or why those thoughts were so strong that they would disrupt her sleep. She also found it amazing that he would imagine her to be so unrestrained. If he knew that wasn't her normal self, would he still want her? She also recognized what he had been doing, because she had experienced all the sensations that he had through this wondrous, disturbing connection they now shared. Yet something had caused him to pull back, to stop before reaching the release he'd obviously been seeking.

Another bright flare of light drew Selene's attention toward the curtained doors, and so did the shadowy figure moving across the veranda. A storm was brewing on the horizon, and someone was outside her room. She suspected she knew the identity of that *someone*. Still, she had to know, had to confirm that before she could rest.

On wobbly legs, she left the bed, tiptoed to the doors and opened the curtains ever so slightly. She discovered him standing at the railing only a few feet away staring off into the distance, his arms crossed on the ledge, his leg bent at the knee, his foot propped on the bottom rail. The occasional flash of lightning revealed the finer points of his form turned slightly profile to her—beautifully naked and a wonder to behold. A steady rain began to fall and still he didn't move, seemingly unconcerned with the light show playing out above him. Rivulets of water gathered on his skin and slid down his body—over the coil of muscle on his bicep, down the path of his spine and the curve of his buttocks. He turned his face up, slicked both hands through his hair and let the rain wash over him, as if engaged in some kind of cleansing ritual.

Selene continued to be transfixed by the image he created against the turbulent skies…until he looked back at her. As if he'd ordained it, another bolt of lightning illuminated his face.

In that moment, she noted the flash of remorse in his beautiful face. She also saw the hunger in his eyes. The desire. And Selene feared she saw something else she might not welcome. Her destiny.

Four

For the past two mornings, Selene had waited until she'd heard Adrien leave his room before she got out of bed. Waited until she was certain she wouldn't have to face him before she took her morning bath and headed downstairs. She hadn't seen him at all since their encounter in his office, or since he'd occupied her mind, and she thought that was probably best for the time being.

Today Ella had left a note stating she had gone into town and would be out until that evening, allowing Selene some privacy to make a call she'd needed to make for a while now. After closing herself in the small office off the kitchen, she withdrew her cell phone from the pocket of her jeans and keyed in the number.

When her sister answered with a cheerful, "Hello," Selene released the breath she'd been holding.

"It's me, Hannah," she said.

"It's about time you called. I've been worried sick about you."

"I'm sorry. I've been busy." Busy trying to keep her brain above water and out of the clutches of the master of the house. "Are you feeling okay?"

"Other than I've got an extra ten pounds sitting on my bladder, I have another couple of weeks before I deliver this kid and Mother is still upset that I'm having the baby at home, I'm fine. Now it's my turn. Where the hell are you, Selene?"

Her little sister was nothing if not direct. She'd been that way for as long as Selene could remember. "I'm in Louisiana. I have a job—get this—at a plantation."

"Doing what? Sending out invitations to parties?"

Selene might have resented Hannah had she not said it in such a teasing tone. "Very funny. I'm overseeing the house's restoration from top to bottom."

After a long silence, Selene asked, "Are you still there, Hannah?"

"Yes, I'm still here. I'm just trying to picture you gainfully employed. Didn't the jackass leave you enough money to survive?"

"He left me plenty of money. A nice check every month. And I need the job because I need to be my own person. I thought you'd understand that."

"I do understand that, Selene. Mother, on the other hand, doesn't. You need to give her a call and explain so she'll quit bugging me."

Their mother understood little beyond untimely disruptions of her social calendar, and that was one phone call Selene would put off for as long as she could. "I will eventually. In the meantime, tell her I'm fine and I'll be in touch. I just wanted to let you know I'm still alive and kicking. And to make sure you're okay."

"I'm wonderful. Doug's been great. He treats me like a queen. I have no real complaints."

Selene had secretly envied Hannah's relationship with Doug. The man had been a saint during his and Hannah's five-year marriage, even though their mother and father hadn't approved of Hannah's choice—a man whose blood was lacking a certain shade of blue, but not his collar. A car mechanic, no less. Dear, rebellious Hannah, who'd always gone after what she wanted, and who'd had the temerity to ignore their parents' ideas on what constituted a good match for their daughters. If only Selene had been so strong. If only she hadn't kowtowed to their insistence that she and Richard take the next step, before Selene had been ready. Come to think of it, she had never really been ready.

"I'll definitely be home for the baby's birth, Hannah. Just give me time to get there if you can."

"Great, and Selene, just one more question. Are you happy?"

Selene rarely asked herself that question these days, or over the past few years, if the truth were known. "Yes, right now I'm happy. For the first time in a while, I feel free."

"I'm glad." Hannah sounded as if she truly was. "But I hope you finally decide to take a few chances, make a few friends. Maybe even meet a man."

Selene released an abrupt laugh. "It's only been a year since I got rid of one man. Why would I want another one so soon?"

"You don't have to marry him," Hannah said. "It's just nice to have a guy around for other things."

Those other things had weighed heavily on Selene's mind over the past few days, thanks to Adrien Morrell. "Actually, I've met someone."

"Wow! Who?"

"The plantation's owner," Selene said. "He's very nice looking although he's somewhat mysterious."

"Nice looking is good. Mysterious is really good. Have you two done it yet?"

"We haven't done anything yet." With the exception of the kiss and the shared fantasy. "I'm only saying that I find him interesting. Nothing may come of it at all." And that was likely considering Adrien's continued absence.

"You should make something come of it," Hannah said. "You've been lonely for too long, Selene."

How well Selene knew that. Yet she had the feeling that even if she did take a few chances with Adrien, she might still be lonely. Worse, she might even be in danger of many things, the least of which was getting her heart crushed. "Look, Hannah, I've already made one mistake with Richard. I don't want to make another. So don't get your hopes up."

Hannah released a long sigh. "Don't be so cautious, Selene."

"What's wrong with being cautious?"

The door creaked open right before the very deep, very clear male voice said, "Because playing it safe isn't very rewarding."

Selene's grip tightened on the cell phone, her mind unable to register what her sister was saying. When she didn't respond, Hannah asked, "Are you still there?"

"Yes, but I have to go now. I'll call you next week."

After saying goodbye and hanging up, Selene swiveled the chair around to find Adrien filling the doorway, wearing a tailored white shirt, plain black slacks and a half smile.

"I was beginning to believe you were permanently living in your office," she said in a slightly unsteady voice.

"I only come out when I have something important to do."

"And what would that be?"

"Another adventure. With you."

Selene wasn't certain she could handle any more of his kind of adventure, especially after the one she'd experienced two nights ago, both in his study and in his mind. "Give me the details and I'll decide if I'm interested."

He leaned his shoulder against the doorjamb. "Did you finish reading the diary?"

"Yes, but there wasn't very much left."

"I know. I've read it. But that doesn't mean other journals don't exist."

"You have more?"

"No, but I know where the cabin is. We might find one there."

"Where is it?" Selene's eagerness came out in her tone, despite the fact she didn't want to seem too excited, even if she was.

He favored her with a slow smile. "It's at the back of the property, next to the swamp. I can take you there."

Selene definitely wanted to see it, but she wasn't sure that was wise. At least not with him tagging along, bringing with him a surplus of sensuality. "If you'll just point me in the right direction, I'm sure I can find it myself."

"I want to show you the way."

She had no doubt he did, and no doubt that he could show her many things. Make her feel things she'd never felt before, if she gave him any indication she wanted that from him. But did she?

Don't be so cautious, Selene....

Maybe Hannah had been right. Maybe she was too cautious. Perhaps that caution had prevented her from knowing the best things in life. And no maybes about it, she was tired of playing it safe. As long as she kept a cool head, remained in control, she could avoid any emotional entanglement.

After pushing back from the desk, she came to her feet.

"I'd love to go with you, but I still have a few things I'd like to do today."

"So do it." He pushed away from the door. "I'll meet you at the back door at five this afternoon."

"Fine. I'll be there."

He turned and walked away, leaving Selene to ponder her decision, and definitely to question her sanity.

Standing at the kitchen door, Adrien Morrell looked like every teenage girl's fondest dream—and every over-protective father's worst nightmare. He wore a black T-shirt cut off at the sleeves that revealed his "power" tattoo, his thumbs hooked into the pockets of a pair of jeans that were faded in several notable places. His air of confidence was palpable, his raw sensuality undeniable. Selene wanted to run—straight into his strong arms. She cautioned herself to remain tough, although that seemed incredibly difficult when he smiled.

As Selene approached him, he gave her a long once-over and a disapproving stare. "That's not a good idea," he said.

Selene frowned. "What's not a good idea?"

"Your choice in clothes."

She looked down at her beige thin-strapped tank top, denim shorts and sneakers before glancing at him again. "It's hot outside. And my feet are sufficiently protected."

"It's rough terrain. Plenty of briars and poison ivy along the way to attack your bare legs."

Obviously she wasn't cut out for this outdoor stuff. "I'll go change into something more appropriate."

"We don't have much daylight left." He opened the door and held back the screen. "You'll have to manage. I'll help you."

Selene brushed past Adrien and he remained behind her as they descended the three steps. Once they reached the overgrown yard, he moved to her side as they walked the well-marked path leading to the swamp. The clearing soon gave way to thick underbrush and twisted trees that hovered overhead, filtering out some of the sun, but not the heat. Because of the recent intermittent rain, the atmosphere was almost unbearable, at least for Selene. Adrien didn't seem to be at all affected by the high humidity and the stifling steam that rose from the soggy ground. He remained silent, staring straight ahead as if deep in thought.

Selene watched her feet, careful not to come too close to anything that looked poisonous or pointy. When the scrub grew thicker, that proved to be a challenge, and that challenge led to a few scratches around her ankles while she fended off several mosquitoes attacking her limbs. But she refused to complain about the bugs and the briars. Refused to come off sounding like some kind of spoiled ninny who didn't have the fortitude to take on the elements. She could deal with a few bites and scrapes for the sake of seeing a part of the past. She couldn't avoid the thornbush that seemed to reach out and grab her leg, leaving a nice long welt down her calf, prompting her to hiss out a breath between her gritted teeth.

Without warning, Adrien swept Selene up in his arms before she realized he'd moved. A sharp gasp left her parted lips and she clung to his neck, immediately noticing the breadth of his shoulders and the dampness beneath the soft curls at his nape.

"This really isn't necessary," she said. "I was managing okay by myself."

"You were getting cut to shreds. Now shut up and enjoy the ride."

Shut up? He'd actually told her to shut up? If he didn't look like a veritable god, she might have slugged him.

A glint of gold where her forearm met his neck caught

her attention. Taking a chance, she kept one arm draped around his neck and used her free hand to pull the chain out from beneath his shirt to study the medallion. "What's this?"

He kept his gaze centered on the trail. "It's a Chinese talisman. The symbol of the snake."

She couldn't resist rolling her eyes. "No doubt, it has some sort of phallic significance."

He sent her a brief glance. "Actually, it symbolizes intuition and perception. And strengthens willpower."

Selene decided she could use a bit of willpower now, especially when he leveled his gaze on her. Only then did she notice his eyes seemed to darken in the daylight, taking on a more cobalt hue. When he turned his profile to her, she also noticed the near perfection of his face, the golden cast of his skin and the temptation of his mouth. She had the strongest urge to reach out and touch his lips, to see if they were as soft as she remembered. Only she didn't care to use her fingertips. She wanted to use her own lips.

"We're here," he announced before she gave into temptation.

Selene tore her gaze away from Adrien's face to see the small log cabin set out in the clearing before them. When they reached the front door, he deposited her back on her feet and released his hold on her—just when she was beginning to enjoy the ride.

He opened the door to a small one-room hut that was dingy and dark even though it was still afternoon. After breezing past her, he opened the heavy shutters on one window, allowing the daylight to stream in. Selene followed his lead, going for another window on the opposite side of the room. As poor luck would have it, the stubborn shutter took a moment to cooperate, and in the process, gifted her with a nice long splinter in her thumb.

"Damn." The oath spewed out of her mouth before she

had the foresight to stop it. She turned to see Adrien smiling at her—a very amused smile. "What?" she asked as she examined her throbbing thumb.

"I didn't know Southern belles knew those kind of words."

"Actually, I have a book of cuss words. I like to practice now and then."

His grin expanded, taking the sting out of her wound. "Good to know I don't have to watch my language around you. Now let me see that."

She shook her hand as if that might dislodge the splinter. "It's not that bad. I'll get it out when we go back to the house."

"I'll take care of it." He crossed the room and caught her hand, turning her palm up to inspect her thumb. He then reached into his back pocket, pulled out a knife and flipped it open with a twist of his wrist.

It took all Selene's power not to jump out of her cross trainers. "I'd really like to keep my thumb, Adrien."

His gaze shot from her hand to her. "What did you say?"

"I said my thumb comes in handy, so I'd like to keep it."

"Not that. You said my name."

Funny, she hadn't even thought about it. The word had flowed as naturally from her mouth as the curse a few moments before. And considering what they'd been through together two nights ago, they should probably be on a first-name basis. "Isn't that amazing?"

He shook his head slightly before returning to tending to her injury. With little effort, he dislodged the splinter and slid the knife into his back pocket. "You'll live," he said, keeping his eyes leveled on her face and her hand still firmly in his grasp.

"I'm sure I will." Even if her respiration wanted to fail her at the moment. "Can I have my hand back now?"

"Sure."

When he released his grip, Selene distracted herself by

studying the area. A lone wooden cot in the corner near the fireplace and a rickety chair by the far window were the only two pieces of furniture to be found. The floors, like the walls, were made of wood and looked as though they hadn't seen foot traffic in decades.

"Not much here," Selene said as she wandered around the room, surveying the cobweb-covered ceiling. "Do you really think this is the place where our unidentified lovers rendezvoused?"

"What do you think?"

"I suppose it's possible. It's a sharecropper's cabin by a swamp." She strolled to the bed and lifted the flattened feather mattress, hoping to find another journal, but no such luck. "Nothing here."

"No discarded chemise or drawers?"

Selene looked up to find him smiling again. She definitely liked his smile. She liked everything about him at the moment. "No. And no journal either. The mystery continues." She straightened and sighed. "I'll just have to search harder. Maybe go into town and see if anyone knows the story."

He leaned his back against the far wall. "You do that, but you might be disappointed with what you learn."

"True. Maybe it's best I don't know. Then I can go on believing they had this grand, passionate affair. Sometimes the fantasy is better than the reality anyway."

"Not always. When two people have enough heat between them, the reality is always better."

Selene was definitely heating up, both from the musty, unventilated cabin and that unmistakable take-me look in Adrien's eyes. "I wouldn't know about that."

Needing some air, she strode to one window and stared out over the marshy terrain. Changing the subject seemed wise. As it was, she'd already said too much. "I think I see some kind of pond in the distance. You know, if this acreage was cleared out, and this cabin restored, it could provide a nice secluded guesthouse for a couple wanting to escape. Before the passion goes away completely." Her cynicism was definitely showing.

She heard the sound of Adrien's footsteps and sensed he was close. He confirmed that when he asked, "You didn't have any passion in your marriage?" from immediately behind her.

She opted not to turn around even though she decided to be honest. "Not exactly."

"Then he didn't do it for you?"

"I didn't do it for him." Too much honesty, she decided. Too much laid bare for him to take the bait.

And he did when he said, "He told you that's why he cheated on you."

Now who was reading whose mind? "Yes, he mentioned that." Right after she'd tapped into Richard's thoughts only to see another woman residing there. A woman who "did it" for him.

Adrien's hands coming to rest on her shoulders sent a pleasurable succession of shock waves along her nerve endings despite the disturbing conversation. "Did he ever encourage you?"

No, but she had tried to encourage him—from intimate meals to sexy lingerie. Eventually, she'd given up. "Define *encourage*."

He breezed his fingertips up and down her bare arms. "Did he ever make love to you in a dark alley after midnight?"

Had it not been for Adrien's close proximity and heady strokes on her flesh, she might have laughed. "Heavens, no."

"He never made love to you in a car in your driveway because he couldn't wait to get into the house before he had you?" He moved flush against her back, wrapped one arm around her middle and breezed his fingertips along the side of her exposed neck. "He never arranged for a private dining room in an exclusive restaurant, then touched you beneath the table until you wanted it right then, right there?"

Selene was certain Adrien had done all those things with a lover, maybe several, even though she couldn't channel his thoughts at the moment. But she could imagine doing all those things with him, and more. "Richard's not that resourceful."

"Richard's a damn fool."

He wouldn't get any argument from Selene on that point, but he did manage to extract a slight shudder when he stroked his knuckles above the rise of her breasts, back and forth in a sultry rhythm. She closed her eyes and absorbed the sensations, leaving her mind open for his thoughts, his fantasies. Yet she saw nothing other than white light, heard nothing but the lyrical cadence of his voice as he continued to speak to her in a steady, stimulating tone.

"We all have the capacity to reach incredible heights during sex." He slid one strap off her shoulder and brushed his warm lips down the bend of her neck before bringing his mouth back to her ear. "You only have to be open to the possibilities."

He lowered his palm to her breast and softly, slowly circled his fingertip around her nipple through the thin knit. Only then did she choose to open her eyes, to watch what he was doing, and she wasn't at all sorry. "This is only one erogenous zone, Selene," he said. "There are a lot more all over your body. Even so, just this little bit of fondling has you hot, doesn't it?"

Selene could do no more than nod her affirmation. Speaking seemed completely out of the question, especially when Adrien slid his palm down to the waistband on her shorts. "Right here, right now, you want me to touch you everywhere." He toyed with the button on her fly, twisting it slightly, torturing her with anticipation. "You want me to take these off you and find out how hot you really are."

Yes, she wanted it. Wanted it more than anything she'd wanted in a long time, even her hard-won freedom. So much so she thought she might actually beg him to do it. But instead of answering her silent plea, Adrien turned her around and readjusted her straps. When she gave him a look of confusion, he simply said, "Not here. At least not now. Tonight."

Selene hugged her arms close to her middle to fend off the unexpected chill. "I'm not sure that's what I want."

He inclined his head and surveyed her face. "You want it as badly as I do, and you know it." He reached over and tucked a random strand of hair behind her ear. "But I'll give you time to think about it between now and then. Think about what it's going to be like with us."

He did no more than draw another line with his fingertip down her throat to her cleavage and back up again along her jaw. But it was enough to make Selene lose all sense of reason. Enough to cause her to wrap one hand around his nape and bring his mouth to hers. He let her take the lead, let her explore, cajole, taste and tempt him. He kept his hands loosely about her waist for a time but as the kiss grew deeper, he moved closer until their bodies meshed together. Until every curve and crevice fitted perfectly against the other, practically interlocked like a human puzzle.

When he pressed one hand on her bottom, bringing her in maximum contact with his erection, and ground his hips against her, she ran her hands up his back beneath his shirt just so she could feel his bare flesh. And she did feel it, every amazing inch of corded muscle, his smooth skin hot and damp beneath her palms. She wanted his shirt gone. She wanted all his clothes gone, and hers, too. She wanted him to lay her down on that ancient cot and thrust inside her, as he had in his fantasy. As the mysterious Z. had taken his lover all those years before. She wanted to know if the reality would be as remarkable, even though she instinctively knew it would.

Without any warning, Adrien broke the kiss and wrested out of her arms. He ran both hands through his hair and then laced his fingers behind his neck. "We need to go now. Before I change my mind and take you right where you stand."

Selene tugged at the hem of her top. "That's probably a good idea."

He sent her a half smile. "Taking you where you stand?"

Oh, yes. Definitely. "Going back to the house before we both do something we regret."

"I promise you, Selene, you won't have any regrets after I'm done with you."

With that, he headed toward the door and Selene followed him outside, her mind whirling with all the possibilities. This time he didn't carry her, but in a welcome display of chivalry, he did take her hand as he navigated the path, kicking aside any rogue limbs and thorns that might reach out and grab her.

Once they made it to the back door, he tugged her back against him, formed one hand to her jaw, and kissed her again, but only briefly. "I want an hour of your time, Selene. Tonight. After it's over, you'll know your own body like you've never known it before. You'll also know the lack of passion in your marriage wasn't your fault."

Then he disappeared into the house, leaving Selene alone to ponder exactly what she was falling into, aside from Adrien's sensual snare. Vigilance came calling, along with a voice that implored her not to be too hasty. Not to listen to her carnal needs. Not to throw out all her caution.

But her sister's voice telling her not to be so cautious drowned out all the warnings. Tonight, she would give Adrien an hour and hope that she came away with all that he'd promised, and more. Why wouldn't she? After all, he was a master of seduction.

"You summoned me, oh master of the household?"

Adrien spun his chair around from his computer to find Ella standing before the desk. "Yeah. I just spoke with your brother. He's expecting you tonight."

Confusion showed in her expression and resonated in her tone when she asked, "Since when?"

"Since I told him you were coming to visit for a few days. I've arranged for a driver to take you to the airport and the plane will be waiting. You can leave immediately after dinner."

"But—"

"No buts, Ella. You haven't seen him in almost two years."

Ella narrowed her eyes. "What are you up to, Adrien?"

He leaned back in his chair and stacked his hands behind his head. "I'm not up to anything. I'm giving you some time off to be with your family. I know you wouldn't go before now because you had this crazy idea I shouldn't be alone. Now you can go without having to worry about me."

She tapped a finger against her chin. "I see. Since Selene's here, you won't be alone."

"That's correct."

The suspicion didn't subside from her face. "Then I take it you two are getting along well."

Damn well, and he planned to get to know her better later this evening. "I'm getting used to her being here."

She propped both hands on her hips and took on her

motherly stance. "I know what you're up to. I see it in your face. You're going to use that charm of yours to seduce her."

If he lied, she would know. Glossing over his intentions seemed the best alternative. "What I do is my business. You don't have to concern yourself."

"I am concerned, Adrien. She's a nice woman. You need to be careful, otherwise she'll be just another one of your casualties."

Adrien could see that she regretted the comment the moment it left her mouth. "I'm not going to force her to do anything she doesn't want to do," he said.

"You don't have to force her. All you have to do is look at her a certain way and she'll follow you anywhere you want her to go. She's vulnerable."

"She's tougher than you think." Tougher than Adrien had first assumed, and he liked that about her. "Now go pack a bag."

"Anything else?" she asked in an overly sweet voice. "Perhaps draw you a bubble bath, light a few candles after I prepare your dinner?"

"That's not necessary. We're only having dinner together." And that's all Ella needed to know right now. He did have a few more plans, but he didn't require candles or warm baths to execute those. He only needed Selene's trust, and he planned to have it tonight.

Ella released a long-suffering sigh. "Okay. I admit it, I'm looking forward to seeing my brother and my nephews." She pointed a finger at him. "But I'm only going to stay the weekend."

"Stay a week, Ella. Or two. You deserve it."

"But—"

"That's an order."

She held up her hands in surrender. "Fine." She left out the door, letting loose a string of Cajun oaths directed at him.

Now that the plan was in motion, Adrien only had to set the stage, beginning with dinner. And after dinner, he intended to keep Selene occupied for at least an hour, if not longer.

Five

Selene was surprised to find the evening meal set out in the formal dining room, not at the small dinette in the kitchen. But she was even more shocked to see Adrien seated at one end of the rectangular table, wearing a crisp white shirt that matched the tablecloth, his dark hair framing his shadowed jaw in soft waves. His very first appearance at dinner.

When she noticed only one other place setting aside from his, she asked, "Is Ella not joining us?"

"She's already had her dinner." He picked up a knife and ran his fingertips along the blunt end of the silver blade. "She's about to leave."

Another surprise among several, and one Selene wasn't certain she welcomed. "Where is she going?"

"Why don't you ask her?"

"I will."

Once in the kitchen, Selene found Ella sliding two

plastic containers inside the refrigerator, a lone paisley bag set out on the floor not far way. "Going somewhere?"

Ella straightened, closed the door and faced Selene with a smile. "To visit my brother and nephews in Shreveport. I'm about to leave as soon as I finish up here. A car's waiting to take me to the airport."

"When did you decide to do this?" Selene heard uneasiness in her voice and tried to temper it when she added, "I don't remember you mentioning a trip."

Ella grabbed a dish towel, wiped her hands and then tossed it aside. "That's because I only decided to go this afternoon."

"Not a family emergency, I hope."

"No, dear, just a visit that's long past coming. I'll only be gone a week, maybe two."

A week or two? Selene resisted wringing her hands from a nervousness she couldn't control. In a matter of moments, she would be in the house with Adrien, completely alone. That created some more cause for concern, although admittedly the thought excited her. "When you return, we need to discuss some of the particulars on the restoration. I have a few ideas I would like to run past you."

"I look forward to it." She picked up the bag and gestured toward the refrigerator. "I've prepared several meals for you to heat up. Just make sure he eats on occasion. He's lost too much weight as it is. He's too thin."

Granted, Adrien was lean, but Selene wouldn't exactly describe him as *thin*. Not in the least. "I'll try, but I don't know if I'll make much headway."

"All I ask is that you try. The rest is up to him." Ella patted Selene's cheek. "Now see me to the door, then you can eat before it gets cold."

Silently they walked past the dining room where Adrien

was still seated, then through the angel rotunda and into the vestibule. At the front door, Ella turned to Selene, concern calling out from her eyes. "Remember what I've told you. Stand your ground with Adrien. Don't let him talk you into anything."

Selene clasped the hem of her blouse and held it tightly. "You don't have to worry. I'm not one to do anything I don't want to do." Not in this lifetime. Not any longer.

"And you don't have to worry about Adrien doing you any harm."

"That's good to know." When Ella's gaze drifted away, Selene's worry increased. "What is it you're not telling me, Ella?"

"He is a very persuasive man, *shâ*. Many a woman could attest to that. But no one knows the real man behind that steel exterior. Take care to protect your heart."

Selene released a humorless laugh. "Believe me, Ella, falling in love is the last thing on my mind. Let's just say I'm rather jaded when it comes to that sort of thing."

"Falling in love isn't always a terrible thing." Ella studied Selene a moment longer, looking thoughtful. "But now that I think about it, you could be the one."

"The one?"

"The one who saves him from his isolation. Saves him from himself, in a manner of speaking. It will take a strong woman, but you could be that woman."

After a brief hug, Ella walked out the door, leaving Selene to analyze her assertions. She'd never seen herself as being all that tough, at least not in recent years. Yet it had taken a good deal of strength to walk away from the only home she'd known and set out on her own. But was she strong enough to prevent her emotions from overtaking good sense if she did become further involved with Adrien?

He is a very persuasive man.... Many a woman could attest to that....

All along, Selene had acknowledged she would be only another conquest. Another woman among heaven only knew how many more. But then, if she viewed it logically, he could be her conquest, too. Her ticket to the adventure of a lifetime. For that reason, she intended to explore all the possibilities with him, beginning tonight. She could play it safe and always wonder what she might be missing, or she could gain firsthand knowledge of his skill as a lover. She wanted that firsthand knowledge. She wanted to know what it would be like to have a man pay complete attention to her needs, as she knew he would.

Driven by anticipation and adrenaline, Selene made her way back through the house at a fast clip. She only paused to take a brief look at Grace's portrait, questioning again if the young woman had been, in fact, the journal's author. If so, Selene could definitely relate to how Grace had felt when she'd met her mysterious lover—excited, winded and somewhat wicked. Which would make Selene a "wanton," she supposed. Well, not yet anyway, but possibly before the night was over, if all went as planned.

When she reached the dining room, Selene discovered Adrien had waited to begin eating. She took her designated place at the opposite end of the table and draped the napkin in her lap.

"Looks great," she said as she inspected the food—blackened fish, a vegetable medley and rice. Unfortunately, she wasn't at all hungry, even though she probably should be.

"Did you and Ella have a nice chat?"

Selene looked up from the plate to find Adrien staring at her. "We didn't really have a chat. I told her to have a nice time and she told me to make you eat." She picked up her fork and gestured toward his plate. "So eat, otherwise

I might be out of a job if she comes back and finds you've totally wasted away."

"I won't be wasting away. In fact, I've had an increase in my *appetites* in the past few days."

Selene concentrated on eating while considering he'd said "appetites," meaning those not only having to do with sustenance. Needless to say, hers had improved as well, but not when it came to this particular meal. The fish was a bit too spicy for her taste and, although the vegetables were good, the rice seemed to stick in her parched throat. For the most part, she pushed the food around on her plate while the silence continued.

"I'm finished," Adrien said after a time, drawing her attention to find his plate absent of any food.

Selene nudged her plate away and dabbed at her mouth with the napkin before setting it aside. "I'm finished, too."

He leaned forward and studied her half-full dish. "You didn't eat much at all."

"It's the hot weather," she said. "I'm never that hungry in the summer."

Without saying a word, he pushed back from the table, stood and strolled toward her, his gaze fastened firmly on hers.

Selene braced for what he might do next until he picked up her plate and said, "I'll be back in a minute. Don't go anywhere."

She wasn't sure she could move even if she'd wanted to.

Adrien grabbed his own plate, headed for the kitchen, then returned a few moments later with an open bottle of red wine. He came back to her, filled the glasses he'd brought with him and set one before her.

She waved it away. "No thanks."

He nudged the wine closer. "Take it. You look like you could use a drink."

Selene decided not to argue since a little libation might not be such a bad idea. Maybe it might even untangle the nervous knots in her belly. "Okay, I guess I could have a glass." Or two or three should she decide she needed to find courage in a bottle. Ridiculous. She didn't have to get drunk to enjoy Adrien's attention. He was already intoxicating enough, particularly the way he filled out his slacks, something she couldn't help but notice when he turned away to reclaim his place at the opposite end of the table.

After he settled back into his seat, he took a long drink of the port before he asked, "What were you like as a child?"

She wasn't expecting that at all. "Serious, I guess you could say. An above-average student. I was fairly reserved." And different, something she'd recognized at a very young age, thanks to the "gift."

He rubbed a hand along his jaw. "Interesting. I had you pegged as a social butterfly."

She'd never quite left her cocoon, the one she'd weaved for self-protection. "Not really. Now my baby sister, on the other hand, was quite the hellion. Someone had to keep her in line."

That seemed to pique his interest. "Are you and your sister still close?"

"Yes. Very close. She's back in Georgia and about to have her first baby. Do you have any siblings?"

He drank the last of his wine and set the glass down hard. "No."

Selene sensed that was somewhat of a sorry subject from the somber look on his face. "What were you like growing up?"

He flashed a wry grin. "Trouble."

She couldn't help but return his smile. "Why does this not surprise me?"

He rimmed a slow finger along the edge of his glass,

drawing her attention. "Unlike you, I wasn't a great student. You could label me the classic underachiever, at least during high school. I did manage to obtain an MBA from Notre Dame."

Selene didn't consider that an underachievement at all. "I went to the University of Georgia for my undergraduate studies. No master's although I did consider going back at one time. But then I made that fatal mistake of getting married instead."

"To Richard the fool."

Selene wrapped both her hands around her glass and stared into the burgundy liquid. "Yes, to Richard the fool."

She heard the scrape of his chair but failed to look up, her pulse accelerating with the sound of his approaching footsteps. She finally did give him her attention when he pulled her chair from the table, turned it to one side, then positioned another chair to face her and dropped down into it.

He rested his hands on her thighs. "I like what you're wearing tonight," he said in his chill-inducing voice.

"Thank you." She'd actually chosen the sleeveless red silk blouse and black mid-thigh skirt for him, as absurd as that seemed.

He inched his hands higher, just beneath the hem. "Have you thought about what I proposed earlier?"

She sighed. "That's all I've been thinking about."

"And?"

"I need to think a little more." As if she could really think at all with his hands on her. "I'll do that while I'm washing the dishes."

"The dishes can wait."

"I need something to do while I think."

He hinted at a smile, as if he might have a suggestion on what she could do. "Leave your veranda doors open in your bedroom. I'll come to you." He leaned over and brushed a soft kiss on her lips, then stood.

"I guess I'll see you in a while, then." She'd agreed without hesitation, but then she'd known all along she would. Known that buying more time would only delay the inevitable, and he knew it, too.

He turned away briefly before facing her again. "Don't get undressed. Wear what you're wearing now."

"Anything else?" she asked.

"That's it. For now."

Then he was gone, leaving behind his sandalwood scent and leaving Selene with a heightened sense of excitement and impatience.

Whatever he had in store for her, Selene doubted she would easily forget it—and she hoped she didn't regret it.

Twenty minutes later, Selene walked into the darkened bedroom, fumbled for the lamp on the dresser and switched it on. After slipping off her sandals, she crossed the room, the floorboards creaking beneath her bare feet, her knees practically knocking from nervousness. She knew what she was about to do would be deemed risky, the reason why she hesitated when she clasped the brass handles. As soon as she opened the doors, she would be opening herself up to several possibilities that could be very good, or very bad, at least in the long term. The long term didn't matter. Being with Adrien tonight did. A risk she planned to take.

Selene opened the doors wide, letting in a draft of warm, humid air. The moon had returned, fuller this time, washing the veranda in a blue glow. She backed away, uncertain what to do next or where to go. Should she lie back on the bed? Or would that make her seem too eager? After deliberating a few moments, she turned off the light, took the wing-back chair across the room and waited. And waited...

Just when she decided Adrien had changed his mind, he appeared at the open doors, causing Selene to startle even though she'd been staring at the spot for several minutes. He moved into the room like some ethereal being. A dark, imposing presence.

Surprisingly, he strode to the dresser and clicked on the same lamp Selene had turned off. Obviously he didn't prefer darkness in every instance. He still had on his slacks, but he'd removed his shirt, and his wavy hair looked as untamed as his eyes. He touched the gold medallion hanging against his bronzed chest then ran a slow palm down from his sternum to his belly. For a minute she thought he might remove his pants but instead, he stalked toward her.

With great effort, Selene maintained a relaxed posture despite the rapid beat of her heart. "I thought you weren't coming."

Adrien braced both hands on the arms of the chair and leaned toward her. "I had every intention of coming, and soon you will, too."

He topped off the suggestive comment with the hint of a smile that did little to ease Selene's urge to twitch in the chair. She clasped his offered hands and allowed him to pull her up into his arms, against his solid body that radiated heat. When she pressed her palms against his chest, intending to explore, he caught her wrists and held her arms at her sides.

"I'll do all the touching," he told her, his voice impossibly deep.

"Does this mean you expect me to be submissive?"

"Yes."

Nothing new there. She'd played the submissive to Richard, but then she hadn't really cared enough to actively participate. Their married life had involved little more than occasional, perfunctory sex. Although she'd avoided too much analysis during their time together, she realized now that any true passion had been lacking from the beginning. During lovemaking—if she could really call it that—she'd always been detached. At times, even uncomfortable. Yet she sensed that with Adrien, detachment or discomfort wouldn't be an issue.

He glanced behind him toward the bed before bringing his gaze back to hers. "Normally I prefer the unconventional, but I might have to make a few concessions tonight."

She was more than curious and a tiny bit nervous over the possibilities. "What do you consider unconventional?"

He brushed her hair away from her shoulders. "Anywhere other than a bed. But after I get started, you might be too weak to stand."

Weak? She was already feeling weak only imagining the potential in his promise. And in order to see this through, Selene would have to give him her trust. She honestly believed he didn't intend to hold her down and torture her, or at least not any way that would put her in serious jeopardy.

Adrien kept his eyes leveled on Selene while he turned her palms up and kissed each wrist. "You don't have to worry," he said, as if he sensed her concerns. "It's up to you to tell me when to stop or to go." He lifted one of her hands and rubbed her knuckles along his jaw. "Although you'll be saying *go* more than *stop*. *Yes* more than *no*."

Selene appreciated his confidence. In fact, she appreciated everything about him at the moment—the length of his dark lashes, the definition of his incredible mouth, the breadth of his shoulders and the clear-cut control he emitted.

Absolute power.

"First, you need to relax," he said as he took her hand and led her to the open doors, then stood behind her. A chorus of locusts seemed to keep time with Selene's thrumming heart as Adrien circled his arms around her waist and pulled her back against him.

"The swamp is a powerhouse of biorhythms at night." He moved his palm to her neck and rubbed his thumb up and down the column of her throat. "Unlike humans, animals don't fight the force of nature."

"They don't overanalyze, you mean." Selene was proud she could assimilate any thoughts at all with Adrien so close.

"Exactly." He tipped her face back with his fingertips and pressed a kiss on her cheek. "They only consider their natural urges."

Selene decided taking a lesson from nature seemed like a fine idea. Right now she would give up all reason for his attention. The pleasure of his touch. He kissed her lightly, chastely, before pulling away until she sought his mouth again. Twice more he retreated, and each time Selene went back for more. Finally he deepened the kiss, suckling her lips, nipping lightly, exploring meticulously with the soft thrust of his tongue.

So wrapped up in that kiss, it took a moment for Selene to register the waft of warm air on her chest. She hadn't even noticed that Adrien had managed to unbutton her blouse, leaving her red lace bra exposed.

He halted the kiss to rest his lips against her ear. "Are you relaxed yet?"

Relaxed, not exactly. Heating up with every passing moment, definitely. "I'm getting there."

"Good."

When he circled her nipple through the thin lace with his fingertip, Selene's whole body felt as if it might liquefy. She could only imagine how she would react when he finally touched her without any barriers at all.

He slid his hand down her bare midriff and around the skirt's waistband, as he had in the cabin earlier that day.

"Stop or go?" In the instant that she hesitated, he told her, "Don't think too much, Selene. Listen to your body, not your mind."

"Go." The word rode out on a shaky breath that halted altogether as Adrien reached down and worked her skirt up her thighs. When he formed one palm between her legs outside her panties and applied only a slight pressure, her knees practically buckled.

He released a rough, sensuous laugh. "We definitely need the bed."

Again he took the lead, and she followed him back into the room without any real qualms. He seated her on the edge of the mattress and left her to open the screened windows flanking the closed doors, then walked to the middle of the room and pulled the chain that set the overhead fan on high.

He came back to the bed and stood over her. "Take off your blouse and your bra." His voice was a firm command. His steadfast gaze demanded she answer.

As if she had no choice but to do his bidding, Selene slid the gaping top off her shoulders with ease and draped it on the footboard. But when she attempted to tackle the bra's front closure, her hands trembled. Adrien knelt in front of her and gently moved her hands away before effortlessly flicking the bra open, proving he'd done this before. Probably many times, Selene decided. When he leaned forward and touched the tip of his tongue to her nipple, Selene experienced a pleasurable shock to her system and drenching dampness between her legs.

He stood, pulled her to her feet and, after he'd proficiently discarded her skirt, he tossed back the bedspread and sheets. "Stretch out on your back, Selene."

Selene was naked except for her panties, and he was still wearing his slacks. That seemed somewhat unfair. "What about you?" she asked.

"What about me?"

"Aren't you going to get undressed?"

"This is all about you right now."

Well, that was definitely a first in Selene's experience, so she chose not to argue even though she was somewhat disappointed. She doubted that her disappointment would last very long. After climbing into the bed, she laid her head back on the pillow, waiting and wondering what Adrien planned to do next.

Following a long look down her body, he sat, leaned over and braced his palms on either side of her. "I want you to watch what I'm doing."

"I want to close my eyes so I can concentrate." The truth, but only in part. She wanted to remain somewhat disconnected. She wanted to treat this exclusively as a visceral experience, leaving all emotions out of it. She didn't want to become too attached to a man who lived only for the moment.

"If that makes you more comfortable, fine," he said. "At least for now."

Selene closed her eyes when he kissed her again with a highly evocative play of his tongue against hers, driving all reservations from her mind. When he broke the kiss and drew her nipple into his mouth, she absorbed the sensations, savoring every pass of his tongue, every pull of his lips. Then something happened that was both unexpected and enthralling—she could see as well as feel what Adrien was doing through the mystical workings of her mind now joined with his. She could see him skim his hands down her sides at the same time she experienced the slight abrasion of his callused palms. Could see as well as feel him draw a line with his fingertips from her pelvis to her hips before drifting down to bend her knees.

For endless moments he caressed her with delicate

strokes all along her body, from her arms to her feet, leaving nothing untouched. After another stimulating kiss, he used his mouth and tongue to follow the path he'd taken with his hands. He tenderly manipulated places that at one time had seemed inconsequential to Selene when it came to lovemaking. Yet with Adrien, every spot he explored became overly sensitive, as if he had found undiscovered erogenous zones. Undiscovered to her, at least.

And all the while, she watched from his perspective from behind closed lids, taking an erotic journey into his mind, sensing his building excitement as well as her own. By the time he sucked a small patch of skin between her thighs, she was bordering on coming totally undone. And when he clasped the elastic band below her belly, she experienced an undeniable ache and another rush of damp heat between her thighs.

But instead of sliding her panties down, Adrien paused and said, "I want you to hold out as long as you can before you climax."

Selene opened her eyes and met his intense gaze. "I'm not sure I can."

He gave her the most patently sexy look she'd ever witnessed from a man. "Then I guess I'll be forced to give you another orgasm."

This had to be a dream. Never before had Selene encountered a man so determined to give her complete pleasure with no thought of his own needs.

Without wavering, Adrien worked the lace down her legs and tossed her panties aside. Again Selene closed her eyes and saw what he saw as he parted her legs. Now she was completely exposed to him and more vulnerable than she'd ever been before. Yet any concerns she might have entertained gave way to an unqualified rush when he divided her flesh, tested her with a fingertip, then two as he fondled her inside and out. He knew how to tease. He knew how to tempt. He knew exactly where to concentrate his attention until she lifted her hips in response.

Holding back wasn't going to be possible, that much Selene knew as the first contraction hit her, causing her to clasp fistfuls of the sheet. She gritted her teeth, tried to cling to her control, but that control clashed with the need for release. The climax surged through her, shaking her entire body. She tipped her head back and a steady moan threatened to leave her mouth, saved only by Adrien's own mouth closing over hers to absorb the sound.

When he broke the kiss, Selene opened her eyes to find him studying her. She draped an arm over her damp forehead and sighed. "I'm relaxed now."

He released another low, grainy laugh. "You're almost too hot to handle. But I'm going to do it to you again."

"Adrien, I…"

Can't handle any more. She had no choice but to try as Adrien began touching her as ardently as he had before.

"I want to use my mouth on you," he said as he slid a finger inside her. "But I'll save that for later, when I know you're ready."

If he did use his mouth, Selene had no doubt she would dissolve into the mattress beneath her back. And she wasn't concerned with later. She was focused only on the here and now as Adrien worked his spell, speaking to her in a low steady voice, telling her how sweet she was and describing what he was doing to her in very detailed terms. In a matter of moments, he had her back on the brink, ready to plummet again. When he whispered, "I'm going to make you scream," that was all it took.

Selene didn't exactly scream when the orgasm hit, but she did groan. A long, almost mournful groan that she couldn't believe actually came from her. She had no idea what he had done, only that she was practically panting by the time the sensations subsided. Then suddenly Adrien was next to her, enfolding her in his arms, soothing her with gentle kisses on her lips and cheeks.

"Where did you learn to do that?" she finally managed to say.

He brushed her hair from her forehead and kissed her there. "I studied tantric sex. Since then, I've done some modification and experimenting. And I've practiced."

"With several partners, I take it." Something that didn't set well with Selene.

"No. Only a chosen few."

That relieved her somewhat. "Should I be flattered?"

"Yes, you should. I'm very selective. And I always begin with the singular purpose of pleasing a woman. I've only scratched the surface with you."

He'd scratched a few itches she hadn't realized she'd had until now. "I'm not sure I can take much more of that."

He rose up on one elbow, using his fist to support his jaw while keeping his free hand idling on her breast. "You can. But right now, you need to sleep."

Selene could only gape when Adrien left the bed and started toward the door. "Wait a minute. That's it?"

He faced her again. "That wasn't enough?"

"Actually, I thought we were going to…" She wasn't quite sure how to say it.

He leaned back against the door. "Anyone can climb on and have it over in a matter of minutes, Selene. But not everyone takes the time to get to know their partner's body. I want to know yours before I'm inside you. And I'm only getting started."

Then he left the room, the sounds of his footsteps and the opening and closing door echoing in Selene's ears.

Adrien Morrell was a sexual savant bent on demonstrating his genius on her. And she would continue to be a willing study, as long as he eventually gave in and gave her his all.

Six

Selene awoke the next morning, still restless even though she'd slept remarkably well, thanks to Adrien's undivided attention. She couldn't recall the last time she'd been so relaxed, even if she hadn't gotten everything from him that she'd wanted. Hopefully that would be included in the next phase. In the meantime, she had work to do.

She went through every room on the first floor, taking inventory of the furnishings as well as jotting down ideas and making a few preliminary sketches. She wanted to retain as much of the original atmosphere as possible, which meant eventually scouring antique stores to fill in wherever necessary, unless she found more items in the attic. She made a note to explore there in the next few days.

By the time afternoon rolled around, her head began to spin when she considered how much she needed to do with a house this size, including refurbishing the flooring and updating the kitchen. Right now, she needed to get out of the house, if only for a while. She also needed to see Adrien, the reason why she set out for his office before she drove into town.

When she knocked, he called, "Come in," in a gruff voice.

She opened the door to find him standing with his back to her, one hand holding back the curtain as he stared out the window. His white shirt was rolled up at the sleeves and it appeared he might be wearing the same pair of slacks he'd worn last night. Had he slept in his clothes? Had he slept at all?

She cleared her throat to garner his attention. "I'm about to go into town for a while, if that's okay with you."

He let the curtain drop and slowly turned to face her. His rumpled unbuttoned shirt hung open, revealing his incredible chest. "You don't need my permission to leave the house."

She centered her gaze on his coveted medallion resting flush against his chest. "I thought you might have something you need me to do first."

When she forced her gaze back to his face, along came the suggestive look he flaunted so well. "I do, but we'll save that for later." He rounded the desk and leaned back against it. "Unless you're reconsidering after last night."

Selene fumbled in her purse for the car keys, unsuccessful in her first two attempts to find them. "I'm leaving all options open. In the meantime, is there anything you need me to pick up from the store?"

"Do we need condoms?"

She gripped the keys tightly in her palm as a hot blush raided her cheeks. "As far as birth control is concerned, no, I'm on the Pill. But we do have other things to consider."

"I've made more than a few mistakes in my time, Selene, but carelessness during sex isn't one of them. Trust me, you don't have to worry that I have some sort of disease. I wouldn't do that to you."

"The same holds true for me." She had spent several months after she'd tossed Richard out making certain her ex-husband hadn't left her with any reminders of his infidelity, other than bitter memories.

"Good," he said. "When I make love to you completely, I don't want anything between us at all."

"It's nice to know you still plan to make love to me, hopefully before I'm too old to care." Where on earth had that come from? Apparently from that recently discovered area of her brain known as "sex central."

He gave her a smile as he pushed off the desk. "You are an impatient little minx, aren't you?"

She was now. "I should go so I'll be home before dark."

He moved in front of her and drew a line down her jaw with his fingertip. "You want to get home to have more of what you had last night."

Very true, Selene decided. But she wouldn't give him the satisfaction of knowing that. "I was thinking about dinner."

He snagged the belt loop on her jeans and tugged her against him. "To hell you were. You're thinking about sex. About me touching you again. If I said the word, you'd let me take you right here on my desk."

Selene received a very detailed vision of that, thanks to Adrien. She glanced behind him and frowned. "I believe I'll wait."

"Fine, because I have no intention of taking you on a desk the first time."

So long as he took her, Selene didn't care where it happened. She formed her palm to his stubbly jaw. "Do me a favor and shave before tonight."

He moved her hand to his lips and streaked his tongue over her palm before placing it against his chest. "I'll definitely do that. I wouldn't want you to suffer from whisker burn."

"I do have a very sensitive mouth."

His smile was oh so wicked. "I wasn't referring to your mouth."

She backed out of his hold and tugged at the hem of her T-shirt. "I see."

"Not yet, but you will."

"I'm leaving now."

He crooked a finger at her. "Not until you come here."

Selene knew exactly what he wanted and she wanted it, too. A quick kiss goodbye. A prelude to what he had in store for her that evening. She easily moved back into his arms and tilted her face up in a blatant offering of her mouth. Instead of kissing her, he brought his lips to her ear. "If you think you want it badly now, wait until tonight. I'm going to take you places you've never been before."

Only then did he meld his lips to hers, driving her wild with the sweep of his tongue before he released her.

Selene wanted him to take her to those places, wanted him to take her beyond the limit. And that want had her counting the minutes until she again entered Adrien's dark, seductive world.

He didn't show up for dinner. In fact, Selene hadn't seen him since she'd come back to the house from her errand run. After she did a load of laundry and cleaned up the kitchen, she went to her bedroom in hopes of finding him waiting for her, only to find the place deserted.

She opted to take a quick bath and ready for bed before she decided what to do next. Dressed in a mid-thigh pink satin robe, her wet hair bound in a towel, she stepped into the hallway and encountered her least favorite demon. Even after a few days of enduring Giles, her heart leaped into her throat every time she laid eyes on his murderous guise. Tonight she was jumpy enough without having to deal with him. On that thought, she pulled the towel from her hair and tossed it at him, making a perfect three-point landing on his horns and effectively covering his snarl. Unfortunately, the poor terrified woman was still exposed and, unless Selene retrieved a blanket to use as a drape, she would have to ignore her.

She returned to her still-empty bedroom and ran a brush through her hair. On afterthought, she dabbed on a little lip gloss and applied a touch of mascara, just in case she might actually get lucky with Adrien. Now the time had come to execute plan A—make the short trip to his office in hopes she might find him there. She padded down the corridor on bare feet, trying desperately to ignore the rasps and groans of the floor, the darkness down below and the dim light in the hallway.

She stood outside his office for a time, and when a knock received no response, she listened carefully and heard nothing. She tested the handle only to find it locked. Disappointed over her lack of success, she headed back down the corridor and paused at the staircase's landing to look down into the dark depths of the rotunda. She wondered if Adrien was prowling around like some restive creature of the night. Even if that was the case, she had no intention of going outside to find him.

When she reached her room, Selene sent a quick glance at the demon only to find the towel was gone. Either he'd managed to remove it himself—a thought she preferred not to entertain—or Adrien had been around at some point in time.

Maybe it was time for plan B—checking out Adrien's inner sanctum. She stopped outside his bedroom and, after finding the door partially ajar, called his name. When she received no answer, she stepped inside. The room was much bigger than hers, much cooler thanks to an operable window air-conditioning unit, and definitely more opulent.

That didn't exactly surprise her. After all, he was the lord of the manor. A gilded bed, the headboard and footboard upholstered in heavy blue brocade with a matching spread, sat angled in the corner across the room near the doors leading out to the veranda. To the left of those doors, a long Victorian walnut chaise covered in gold damask and two blue-and-gold striped armchairs formed a sitting area lit by a lone brass floor lamp.

Selene noted a door not far from the right of the bed and presumed that was the master bath. It didn't seem wise to try and find out if he might be in there. Of course, she didn't actually have to go in. She could stand by a few minutes and listen to see if he was taking a shower. She crossed the room to investigate and discovered no light filtering through the door, no sound coming from inside, indicating he was somewhere else in the house. But where? She supposed he could have taken a drive, but she didn't recall seeing any car other than Ella's hatchback.

She started to leave but instead turned back to survey the room. She had two more options—wait for him here in hopes he'd eventually come to her, or wait in her own bedroom with the veranda doors opened wide in invitation as she had last night. Or she could explore a bit more, beginning with the locked chamber across the hall. But did she dare? If he happened to be in there and she knocked, he would either allow her in or tell her to go away. He might also be angry over the intrusion. If so, he would simply have to get over it.

Filled with determination, Selene took one last glance at the room then spun around—only to run into a solid wall of prime male.

With one hand against her pounding heart, Selene stepped back to find Adrien dressed in a T-shirt and jeans, his jaw clean shaven, his hair shower damp, his feet bare… and a towel dangling from one hand. Her discarded towel. "Did you lose something?" he asked.

She suddenly felt very silly. "I was wondering where that went."

He slid a slow glance down her body. "I was hoping you were leaving a trail so I could find you."

"Actually, I got tired of that monster leering at me. I took the towel from my hair and covered him up."

"Too bad the towel wasn't around your body."

Selene felt as if she were totally naked now under his perusal as he took a step toward her. "Did you need something from me?" he asked.

He knew exactly what she needed, but Selene wasn't about to bite. "I needed to tell you that the contractor will be here first thing Monday morning to assess the repairs."

"It's only Friday."

"I was afraid I might forget to mention it."

"You were afraid I might not pay you a visit tonight." She shrugged. "Since it's late, maybe some other time."

When she started past him, he grabbed her arm and pulled her around. "It's not too late to give you what you need."

"I don't *need* anything from you." Another tiny lie.

"Okay, what you *want*." He slid his hands inside the collar of her robe and rubbed her neck with his thumbs. "It's already started, the addiction. Don't bother to deny it."

She wasn't a card-carrying Adrien addict yet, but she could be. Which is what made this situation so hazardous. "Look, whether you want to continue this or not is immaterial to me."

"It's everything to you." He clasped her waist and hauled her against him. "Now that you know what you've been missing, it's difficult to do without it."

"I can do without it, thank you very much."

"Are you sure about that?"

She was only sure of one thing—he could do things to her that no man had ever done with only a look.

Without the least bit of warning, he pulled up the back of her robe and ran his hands over her bare bottom. "For someone who doesn't want it, you're certainly prepared to get it."

She shivered slightly despite her efforts to stop it. "I didn't have the opportunity to get dressed after my bath."

"You didn't have any intention of getting dressed after your bath." He took his hands from her bottom and brought them to the robe's sash, releasing it with only a minimal tug. After parting the fabric, he took a step back and a visual excursion down her body that was already flushed. "Now to decide exactly what I'm going to do to you, and where I'm going to do it."

She closed her robe and redid the sash for the sheer pleasure of having him open it again. "I don't remember giving you permission to do anything to me."

He gestured to the door. "Go, then. I'm not going to force you into anything."

Damn him. And damn herself for her inability to resist him. "Well, I suppose since I don't have anything better to do, we could spend some time together."

His smile was smug and tremendously sexy. "That's what I thought."

Clasping her hand, he led her to the chaise and sat her down. Then he took the chair across from her, tugged his T-shirt over his head and tossed it behind him. Selene held her breath when he toyed with his fly before lifting his hand and settling it on his thigh without lowering his zipper.

He was taunting her. And she wasn't going to let him get away with it. "You can take off your pants, Adrien. It's nothing I haven't seen before."

He stretched his long legs out before him and laced his hands atop his belly. "Don't be so sure about that."

A tiny shiver ran up and down her spine. "A bit egotistical, are we?"

"This isn't about ego. It's about your experience." He leaned forward and nailed her with his deadly gaze, the medallion dangling from his neck serving as a reminder of his strength of will. "Have you ever really looked at a man before, Selene? Studied all the details of his body?"

She'd lost her virginity in the dark after a fraternity fling and had married a man who was a lights-out kind of guy. "I guess I would have to say no, not really."

"Then you still have a lot to learn."

"Let's get to it then." Obviously she was suffering from an overdose of enthusiasm.

"Not yet." He slowly rose from the chair and stood before her. "We're going to take this slowly."

"I don't want slowly."

He pulled the sash, parted her robe again and slid it off her shoulders. "You're going to get slowly whether you want it or not. Now recline on the chaise."

Selene scooted up against the angled tufted back and stretched her crossed legs before her, propped her elbow on the rolled arm and draped her other arm across her middle. In a way, she felt like a queen waiting to be tended by a dark, dangerous knight. She found it odd that she didn't feel uncomfortable over being totally nude in his presence, until he continued to stand there, sizing her up like a sculptor preparing to mold his next masterpiece.

In a fit of self-consciousness, she started to fold her arms across her breasts until Adrien said, "Don't you dare cover yourself."

"Okay." Her voice sounded pathetically weak, which complemented the way she felt at the moment.

"You have no idea how beautiful you are, do you?" he asked.

"I've never thought much about it." Other than she'd always believed her nose was too sharp, her hair too thin, her brown eyes too wide set and nondescript. All those little worries that women often obsessed about when things could be so much worse.

He moved a little closer. "Did he ever tell you that you're beautiful?"

She sighed. "I don't understand your preoccupation with my ex."

"Because he's the reason you're unable to let go."

Maybe so, but what were Adrien's reasons? She wanted to ask but she didn't want to anger him and, in turn, send him away. "I was under the impression I let go quite well last night."

"Not completely. And that's what I want from you tonight. I don't want another man in your mind aside from me."

He had no idea how deeply ingrained he'd been in her mind since they'd met. "I can manage that."

"Good. But as tempting as you look right now, there's not enough room for both of us on that damn lounger."

Selene pointed to her left. "There's always the bed."

"And there are other alternatives, too."

Obviously Adrien had an aversion to beds, Selene decided. And to lights, her next thought when he snapped off the floor lamp, sending the room into darkness. When she heard the rasp of his zipper and the rustle of denim, she stopped thinking altogether, her mind caught in the grip of anticipation even though she couldn't see much more than the outline of his body.

"Stand up," he said.

When Selene left the chaise, he clasped both her hands

and held them against his chest. "I'm giving you the chance to learn all the details."

"How can I when I can't see you?"

He took her palm and pressed it against his face. "After last night, you should know the answer to that."

She did know the answer—by using her hands. While Adrien stood there, his arms at his sides, she began by streaming her fingertips along his jaw before tracing a line along his full lips, pausing to briefly touch her lips there. She traveled down the column of his throat, past his Adam's apple, and used her splayed palms to explore his collarbone before roaming down to the solid plane of his chest covered in a slight dusting of hair. When she grazed his nipples, she detected a slight shudder that led her to linger for a while longer before breezing her hands down his sides and over his rib cage.

Deciding to save the best for last, Selene moved behind him and felt her way over his broad shoulders, joining her hands in the middle of his back to follow the path of his strong spine. His skin grew damp beneath her palms and the cadence of his breathing quickened as she discovered the dip below his waist. She fashioned her palms to his buttocks, kneading slightly before following the crevice with her fingertips and curling them between his legs. He opened his stance slightly, allowing her more room to delve as far as she dared, which she did for a time before she touched the backs of his hair-roughened thighs.

She returned to stand before him, taking up where she'd left off, beginning with his rigid abdomen that grew tauter when she touched him. She circled her fingertip around his navel and his breath hitched slightly. Yet he kept his arms dangling at his sides, even when she moved her palms lower to stroke his pelvis, finding the ribbon of hair that created a path leading to all that made Adrien premium male.

But now that the moment she'd been anxiously awaiting had arrived, Selene hesitated, and that was absurd. She'd touched a man intimately before. Why was touching Adrien so different?

"Do it, Selene."

Buoyed by Adrien's demand, in a voice grainy with need, Selene didn't have to journey far before discovering he was definitely aroused. She explored the length of his erection with a slow glide of her fingertip before taking him completely into her hands. She didn't have to ask what he liked, what spots were particularly sensitive to her touch. She only had to open her mind and tap into his thoughts to learn his reaction as she began to caress him with long, fluid strokes. She soon sensed his emergent need, his battle with control. She knew he was nearing the edge and that he would prevent her from continuing a moment before he clasped her wrist and lifted her hand to his pounding heart.

"Stop." Selene heard the effort in that one word, felt his slight tremor.

After Adrien tugged her down to the floor and positioned her on the plush Oriental rug, he left her for a moment to turn on the lamp, the beam illuminating her body like a movie premiere searchlight, and giving her a great view of the places she had touched only moments before. And what a glorious view it was.

He joined her on the rug, propped a throw pillow beneath her neck and lifted her arms above her head. In only a few moments, he had her body weeping for him, trembling for more, and he knew it, apparent by the perception in his dark gaze. When he came to his knees between her parted legs, Selene wasn't sure she could stand the anticipation.

After spending a few moments finessing her breasts with his mouth, he drew a line with his tongue down her torso. And when he went as far as he could go before reaching his ultimate destination, Adrien lifted his head and commanded, "Watch, and don't think."

Selene could do nothing more than watch when he dipped his head between her legs and went on an all-out assault on her body, the kind that would definitely lead to an explosion. She laid her palms on his dark, damp hair as he explored, using his mouth to gain supreme advantage. As good as Adrien had made her feel last night, nothing could match this incomparable intimacy. Nothing. Her gratification only intensified when she opened her mind to him and saw the scene from his perspective, knowing that as he gave her that pleasure, he in turn received pleasure.

Selene could only remain mute and motionless…until he used gentle suckling as his weapon of choice. Her hips bucked when the climax crashed down on her, wresting another long groan from deep within her throat. But Adrien wasn't through yet. With his gaze firmly locked into hers, he paused to blow his warm breath over her sensitized flesh before swooping back in with his clever mouth. He remained relentless with his goal through gentle yet single-minded manipulation. She wanted to beg him to stop. She also wanted more. After the second orgasm consumed her, bringing with it a series of shudders, she clawed at his shoulders and the word "Please," left her mouth in a desperate, pleading tone.

Adrien worked his way up her body and kissed her deeply while she raked her fingernails down his back. He rubbed his chest over her breasts in a deliberate, rhythmic motion while she shifted her hips in encouragement. She sensed his sudden struggle, felt his faltering control and the nudge of his erection between her legs, until his mind went totally blank as if he'd raised a mental fortress to block her out completely.

Without any explanation, he rolled away from her and

stood. Keeping his back to her while he shrugged on his jeans, he said, "That's enough for now. We'll continue this tomorrow."

Selene recognized there was more to his reticence than taking it slowly. Much more. "Then you're saying if I want you to make love to me now, you won't do it?"

He turned, snatched her robe from the floor and tossed it at her. "Not tonight."

She sent a direct look at his fly as she clutched the robe to her breasts. "Are you into masochism or are you trying to prove your strength?"

"I'm patient. I can wait. I also have some work to do."

Selene pulled the robe on and thought back to the night when he'd first invaded her mind. When he'd denied himself then, as well. As he started to leave, she said, "What are you afraid of, Adrien?"

He turned and frowned. "I'm not afraid of anything."

She rose and joined him at the door. "You're afraid you're going to feel something, aren't you? That it won't be only meaningless sex between us." She lined the ridge beneath his slacks with a fingertip. "That has to be it since there's not a thing physically wrong with you."

She saw it then, another slide show coming from his mind—him backing her against the wall, shoving his pants to his thighs, thrusting inside her. But he forced the image away at the same time he took her hand and held it at her side. "I'm not afraid, Selene. But I say when and where we make love. You don't have to understand why I want to wait. You only have to respect it."

She understood all too well. A woman in his immediate past kept him guarded. Most likely, the woman named Chloe who was still influencing him, even if Adrien couldn't admit it to Selene or himself. But Selene didn't dare mention that woman's name, otherwise she would have to explain how she'd come by the information. Right now she would keep her own secrets, and let him have his.

Resigned to letting him have his way, she stepped back and cinched the robe tightly. "Fine. You go ahead and leave now. But remember what I've said before, no power is absolute. I could very well be the one who says when and where."

She knew he still battled with coming back to her, but when he touched the medallion dangling from his neck before turning away again, it became apparent his will-power had won out. At least for now.

After Selene returned to her bedroom, she forged her own plan. She vowed to help Adrien get past his fears and if that meant taking the lead, so be it. She might only be a temporary fix for his problems, a means to help him over the life-altering hurdle that had caused him to retreat. But as long as he didn't turn her away, she believed anything was possible.

Adrien locked himself in the room across the hall to keep from going to Selene to finish what he'd started. He also needed to remember why he couldn't become too deeply involved with her. What better place to do that but in this dark, desolate tomb? The room didn't serve as a shrine; no real reminders of Chloe remained. At least not those that revealed what she had been, and not what she had become.

He walked to the window where she had once stood looking out over the grounds while dreaming of those things that had been outside her reach because of him. He collapsed into a chair by that window and, in the cover of darkness, plagued by the physical pain of needing and not having, he analyzed Selene's conjecture.

He did have fears, all justified. He feared she could be the one woman who would force him to face his downfall, tear open his wounds and make him bleed again. He also recognized she was a woman who under normal circumstances wouldn't interest him at all. But nothing about their liaison was normal. From the beginning, he'd realized she was special, unique in ways he didn't quite understand. He only knew that something about her had drawn him from the moment he'd seen her.

He also recognized the risk in that. A risk he couldn't afford. He'd set a dangerous course the moment he'd touched her, and he needed to halt it soon. Before he did something that they would both regret.

Seven

The following morning, Selene needed something to do other than worry over Adrien. For that reason, she opted to explore the third-floor attic, afforded only a brief glance at Adrien's closed office door and kept right on walking until she located the attic's entry. After last night, she decided she'd been too accessible. Too compliant. The time had come for her to take control.

When she opened the attic door, she encountered another steep staircase and flipped on the switch that turned on a lone bulb hanging high overhead. With each step she took, an ominous feeling assaulted her. She scolded herself for overreacting and continued on, not certain of what she would find. Hopefully not a passel of rodents and spiders. Or wandering spirits.

She opened a second door and entered the area that spanned the length of the house. Although rays of light filtered in from the three dormer windows, the place still retained a gloomy atmosphere, from the weathered wood floors to the cobwebs draped in the corners. A pile of helter-skelter planks and fabric near one window immediately caught her attention, and upon further investigation, she discovered several splintered chairs and tables, as if someone had taken a sledgehammer or hacksaw to them. Someone who obviously didn't like the furniture, or had chosen to expend their anger on the antiques.

A sense of foreboding sent chills up her spine like menacing fingers, and she gladly left the furniture remnants behind to examine the two boxes across the room. She came upon a gold mine—several pieces of fine china and glassware, all carefully wrapped in white cloth, a definite contrast to the destruction. But she found no missing journals, no other pieces of the past. And she wasn't up to searching for more clues at the moment.

After organizing the boxes, Selene left the attic and made her way to the room that Ella had claimed was once the nursery—a happier place, she hoped. She again paused outside Adrien's office door and considered knocking, until she heard the sound of muffled conversation. Apparently he was on the phone discussing business, so she decided not to disturb him. At least not yet.

Selene opened the door to another lengthy room painted a bright yellow, sunshine spilling from the uncovered windows casting golden light on the walls, dust motes floating about like miniature snowflakes. And in the corner rested a tiny spindled cradle and a lone wooden rocking chair that looked as if they'd had limited use. When she crossed the room and nudged the cradle, a strong sense of sadness overcame her. Perhaps this room, too, had been the site of some tragedy, and she hated to think that tragedy involved a child.

A series of shrill rings jerked Selene back into the

present. She pulled her cell phone from her pocket and answered with a melancholy, "Hello."

"Hi, Selene. It's Abby. Are you busy?"

"Not at all. As a matter of fact, I was about to call you. I've found a few pieces of china I'd like you to take a look at when you have time."

"I'll be out of town until the end of next week, but feel free to bring them by then. And I'm calling you because I think I found someone who might be able to help you with the house's history."

The timely twist of fate definitely elevated Selene's optimism. "Who?"

"His name his Jeb Gutherie and he lives in an assisted-living community in Baton Rouge called Briar Oaks. I don't have an exact location, but it shouldn't be too hard to find."

Not much to go on, but Selene was willing to take her chances. If she left now, she could arrive before lunch. And if lucky, she might have at least one mystery solved today. "Thanks, Abby. You've come to my rescue again."

"You're welcome. How's the job going?"

The job was going fine. Her relationship with Adrien was going places it probably shouldn't. "I'm making slow progress, but it's still progress."

"Seen any ghosts yet?"

Only in her dreams, particularly last night. She'd seen Grace's face that had turned into another unidentified face—a woman with light brown hair and vibrant blue eyes. She'd woken up twice, practically paralyzed, before drifting off to sleep only to have more fitful dreams of falling. "No, no spirits. Only the occasional creepy house sound."

"Let me know if anything changes, and good luck."

Following the phone call, excitement over the prospect of unraveling the plantation's past sent Selene out of the house and to her car without telling Adrien goodbye. After all, he'd said she didn't need his permission to leave, and she didn't intend to request it. Having him wonder where she might be going could prove to be a good thing.

He stood at the window and again watched her leave, wondering where she might be going this time. Maybe back to Georgia, although she had no suitcases in her possession. He'd heard her footsteps and had opened his door to see her entering the attic and knew what she'd seen—the result of his fury. Yet she had no way of knowing he'd been responsible for the destruction. No way of knowing why he'd taken out his anger on several priceless antiques, and he didn't plan to tell her.

He had no plans to return to her tonight, either. He needed time to assess his next move. To decide how much farther he would go before he put an end to their liaison. Creating some distance between them would be wise. But his wisdom warred with his desire, and only time would tell if he could stay away from her. Correction, how *long* he would stay away from her.

Little by little, she was wearing him down. Tearing away at his resistance and, if not careful, he'd end up traveling down a road he didn't dare take.

An hour later, Selene pulled into the parking lot at a high-rise retirement community north of Baton Rouge. She entered the foyer and was immediately greeted by a young woman seated behind a reception desk. "Welcome to Briar Oaks. May I help you?"

"I hope so. I'm looking for Jeb Gutherie."

She eyed Selene suspiciously. "Is he expecting you?"

"Actually, no. But I believe he has some information I need." Selene glanced at the woman's name tag. "Tisha, could you tell him I'm inquiring about the history of a plantation in St. Edwards?"

Following a sigh, the young woman slid a clipboard in front of Selene. "If you'll sign in and wait here, I'll see if I can find him."

Selene jotted down her name and waited a few moments until the receptionist returned. "He'll see you," Tisha said. "But I have to warn you, he tires easily and might nod off now and then. And he'll need to be in the dining room in about twenty minutes for lunch."

As long as she could garner some information, Selene could live with that. "I won't keep him too long."

Selene followed Tisha through the vestibule that opened into a large atrium with an open-air dining room to the right and offices on the left. Just beyond that, Tisha stopped at a smaller room and faced Selene. "This is the game room. If you need to speak with him privately, you can use the conference area next door."

Selene peeked inside to find a group of four elderly gentlemen playing cards at a round table. "Which one is he?"

Tisha pointed discreetly. "On the far end facing us."

Selene homed in on the man seated in a wheelchair, his shock of gray hair contrasting with his mocha-colored skin. He wore a neat brown suit and a number of years on his thin face. "The one in the bow tie?"

"That's him. And good luck."

"Thanks."

After Tisha departed, Selene stepped into the room and cleared her throat. "Mr. Gutherie?"

He glanced up from his cards, mischief calling out from his light brown eyes. "Well looky here, boys. I have a guest. And a mighty pretty one at that."

All eyes turned to Selene and, after the rest of the card players muttered polite greetings, Mr. Gutherie said,

"Could you give us some privacy, gentlemen? We'll take up where we left off after lunch." He spoke with Southern sophistication, his voice as clear as the summer skies.

The men pushed back from the table, stood and passed by with greetings and cautions not to believe a word Gutherie said. After they'd filed out, Selene approached the table. "Thank you for seeing me, Mr. Gutherie."

"Call me Jeb," he said as he gave her offered hand a gentle shake. "And forgive me for not standing. My legs don't work well, but my mind's still as sharp as a steel trap."

Selene took the vacated chair next to him and set her purse on the floor beside her. "I'm here about the House of Midnight."

His expression turned somber. "The House of Sunshine, you mean. Or at least that's what it was called a long time ago."

A piece of the puzzle had already fallen into place, and that pleased Selene greatly. "I didn't realize that about the name. In fact, I know very little about the plantation's history, and that's why I'm here." She briefly explained her role in the restoration, and then asked the first question that came to mind. "Someone told me you might know something about the previous owners, specifically a woman named Grace. Her portrait hangs in the rotunda."

"Ah, Miss Grace." He tented his fingers beneath his chin and tapped them together. "She lived in the house a long time ago and died before I was born. But my grandmother spoke fondly of her. They grew up together and remained good friends, even after the war."

"Which war would that be?"

He chuckled. "The Civil War, although it wasn't too civil."

Selene tried to hide her shock but doubted she succeeded. "If you don't mind me asking, how old are you?"

"I've seen one hundred years as of this past May," he said proudly. "Miss Grace was my aunt."

Another surprise among many. "Your grandmother and Grace were sisters?"

"No. Miss Grace and my father were half siblings by Stanton Gutherie, a heartless bastard. He owned the plantation next to Sunshine House and thought he owned everything and everyone, including his workers. My grandmother, Effie, was one of his slaves, orphaned at a young age when her parents died after the war. She had no place to go, so she stayed on at the Gutherie plantation. And when she was only fifteen, Stanton got her with child. That child was my father."

Selene had never expected such a disturbing history. "How did Grace come to live at the plantation?"

His face lit up with remembrance. "Ah, Miss Grace was as pure as her father was evil, according to my grandmother. She fell in love with Zeke Cormier, the owner of Sunshine House and a man Stanton hated. But she defied her father and married Zeke against his wishes."

Now Selene knew the identity of Z. in the journal—Grace's journal. "And your grandmother continued to live with Stanton?"

"Luckily, no. Grace took Effie and my father to live with her after she married."

Jeb went on to explain how Grace had become pregnant two years into the marriage, how Effie had described the pure joy in the house, until Grace passed away from black fever a few weeks before the baby was born, a little boy who perished as well.

Jeb sat back and shook his head. "Mr. Zeke went crazy after that. He painted the house black. He refused to let my grandmother clear out the nursery."

Selene recalled the sad little cradle in the corner. "How awful."

"It only got worse," Jeb said. "Mr. Zeke took to the bottle. He eventually drank himself to death. My grandmother tried to help him, but he wouldn't let her. He did leave her the house when he died." Again his expression softened. "I spent summers at the plantation when I was growing up. Many of my fondest memories are tied up in that place. In the grove at the west of the property, my father built a tree house." He rubbed his chin and looked thoughtful. "I wonder if it's still there."

Selene didn't know, but she would find out. "And your grandmother—"

"Died in a rest home back in the sixties. I owned the house until Giles Morrell bought it in a public auction because I couldn't pay the back taxes. I haven't been back since."

"You probably wouldn't want to see it now," Selene said. "It's in a sad state, but I hope to change that soon."

"I wish you luck."

She took Jeb's hand into hers. "Thank you so much. I don't know how to repay you."

He patted her arm. "Treat the house with kindness, Miss Selene. Bring back the joy and the sunshine."

If only she could promise him that, but unfortunately more sadness resided there, resonating from Adrien, although she still didn't know any of those facts yet. But she hoped eventually to come by that information.

Selene had one last question she needed to ask, although she felt a little foolish. "Did your grandmother ever claim to have seen any ghosts?"

Jeb chuckled again. "She swore she talked to Zeke after he passed until she told him to go to the light and find Miss Grace and their boy child. He supposedly left after that and she didn't see him again. Might seem crazy to some folks, but I believed her."

Zeke accepting the call to glory was definitely good news. Selene had one wounded man to deal with; she didn't need another. Especially a ghostly man. "I don't think it sounds crazy at all."

He gave her a questioning look. "Most people don't believe in the ability to talk to the dead.'"

"I'm not most people, I guess."

"Because you have that ability, too."

"I…" How could she possibly respond without lying to him? "I don't talk to ghosts. Let's just say I have strong intuition."

He gave her hand a squeeze. "Miss Selene, I spent my life as a cultural anthropologist, traveling the world. I've seen things that can't be explained, frightening things. Wondrous things. I also know how cruel people can be when I learned early on the meaning of *quadroon* and *mulatto*. But I also learned that what makes us different only makes us unique, and we should be proud of those differences."

Selene lowered her gaze to their joined hands. "It's difficult though, being different."

He tipped her chin up with one careworn finger. "You will find someone someday who will understand and accept you. A man, I believe. If you haven't already found one."

Had she? No, not Adrien. He would never understand her powers any better than she would ever understand the root of his pain.

Tisha stuck her head in the door and called, "Time for lunch, Mr. Gutherie."

Selene stood and offered her hand to Jeb again. "As soon as I have the plantation back in order, I would love to have you visit, maybe even stay a day or two. I'd be glad to pick you up and drive you."

He gave her a mock frown. "Don't take too long, otherwise I might be six feet under."

She laughed softly. "I have a feeling you'll be with us for a while."

His expression turned serious once more. "Miss Selene, I've buried two wives and two sons. I'm ready to go when the Lord calls me home. But seeing the Sunshine House again would give me a reason to stay a little longer, so I'll just tell Saint Peter he'll have to wait until that happens."

Filled with a fondness for this astonishing man, Selene leaned over and gave him a hug. "You be sure to do that."

She headed to the door but pulled up short when Jeb said, "One more thing, Miss Selene."

She turned and faced him again. "Anything."

"This lifetime passes quickly, until one day we turn around and we've seen a century come and go. That's why it's best not to ignore your destiny."

"I'll remember that," Selene said as she left him with a smile.

And she would, even though she had no idea where her destiny might lie.

"Where have you been?"

Selene set her bags on the kitchen counter, surprised to be greeted by Adrien, who both looked and sounded quite perturbed. He also looked like his usual sexy self dressed in worn jeans and tight white T-shirt. "I've been running some errands," she said as she began to unload the groceries.

"You should have told me you were leaving."

She slid two cartons of yogurt and a bottle of orange juice into the refrigerator, turned and closed the door with a push of her bottom. "I recall you telling me that I didn't need your permission to leave the house."

He took a quick check of his watch. "It's almost nine."

"I didn't realize I had a curfew."

He surveyed the two bags on the counter. "For someone who spent the day shopping, you didn't buy much."

"Actually, I didn't only go shopping today. I met with the man who owned this house before your grandfather bought it."

Adrien looked only mildly curious. "How did you find him?"

"Through a friend. He was very nice and accommodating."

"The friend or the previous owner?"

He sounded jealous, and Selene loved it. "Both. The owner's name is Jeb Gutherie. We had a very nice visit."

"Where did you meet with him?" His tone was laced with suspicion.

She could extend the game, or admit the truth and be done with it. "At the retirement home in Baton Rouge. He lives there."

If Adrien was at all relieved, he didn't show it. "You spent the better part of the day with him?"

She'd spent the better part of the day in a bookstore with a mocha cappuccino, reading a sex manual. She'd also made a purchase that she hoped might prove beneficial later tonight. "I spent less than an hour with him, but I've solved the mystery of our lovers. He told me—"

"Spare me the details."

She shrugged, said, "Okay," and opened the cabinet to put away a few staples. If he was too stubborn to hear the news, she'd save it for later.

"You didn't stop anywhere on your way back?" he asked.

His third degree was getting just a bit tired. "I grabbed some fast food on the way home. Oh, and I stopped at a biker bar and played pool with the locals. I even got a tattoo on my butt. It says Helpless Georgia Peach." She turned from the cabinet and sent him a sunny smile. "Would like to see it?"

His expression turned stony. "I'm glad you find this humorous, but I damn sure don't. Anything could have happened to you on the back roads at night."

She couldn't resist rolling her eyes. "Oh, please. I drove all the way from Georgia alone and that took nine hours, not thirty minutes." She propped one elbow on the counter and leaned into it. "Did you miss me?"

When he didn't respond, she walked right up to him, wrapped a hand around his neck and pulled his mouth to hers. At first he failed to respond, but with a little cajoling, he soon became an active participant in the kiss. She relished the hardness of his body, the play of his tongue and the feel of his palms sliding over her bottom.

But Selene only allowed it for a while before she pulled away and reclaimed her place at the counter. "Well, I guess that answers my question. You did miss me."

He stared at her for a few moments and Selene knew what he wanted to do. Saw what he wanted to do in a series of images, all involving hoisting her up onto the counter and having his way with her right there. But instead of acting on the fantasy, he turned and muttered, "I'm going to bed."

Selene knew better. Maybe he was retiring to his bedroom, but he wasn't going to sleep. And if all went as planned, she would make certain of that.

When she was assured Adrien had gone upstairs, she grabbed the plastic boutique bag and walked quietly to her room, turning down the lights behind her. She'd grown more comfortable with the darkness even though she still dreaded the sounds. Even more so now that she knew Grace's and Zeke's stories. She paused at the top landing and stared down the darkened corridor housing the nursery that had never been used, again overcome with a strong feeling of sadness.

Shaking off the melancholy, Selene headed down the hall, purposefully avoiding the demon's steely glare. She took a quick bath, retired to her room and withdrew the negligee from the sack—a simple short satin slip of a gown, appropriately the color of her mother's Black Magic roses. She could definitely use a little magic tonight, as well as some courage.

After dressing in the gown, she collapsed onto the bed and ran her hand over the silky fabric, bringing about a host of memories of the last time she'd done this very thing with another man in mind, but for all the wrong reasons. As it turned out, Richard hadn't been at all receptive. With Adrien, she might be setting herself up for the same rejection. But she had to try. She'd spent a good two hours that day studying the philosophy behind tantric sex, and in turn realizing what Adrien's "modified" method had been missing—the part that dealt with enlightenment and illumination, and the purity of love. In order to reach that plane, one had to be open emotionally as well as physically. Adrien had avoided emotions altogether. He was still avoiding them.

Selene honestly believed that if she could convince him to let go of his resistance, his control, then maybe his internal wounds might begin to heal. Maybe he could allow himself to feel again. Or perhaps he might close himself off even more.

She wanted to take that chance. Had to take that chance. First, she had to find him, and she hoped that didn't entail searching the entire house.

When she heard the sound of his door opening onto the balcony, she knew that wouldn't be the case. The time had arrived to make her move. To show him that her patience had run out. And to make his fantasy a reality.

* * *

While he sat rigid on the wicker sofa, Adrien knew what Selene wanted the moment she walked onto the veranda. Aided only by moonlight, he could see she wore red, the mark of seduction, and a determined expression. He could also see the paleness of her skin set against the night sky, the way her golden hair curled around her shoulders like a halo. An angel bent on seducing the devil himself.

Not once had he ever passed up the opportunity to make love to a willing woman. Not once had he ever denied himself for such a long period of time since he'd discovered the benefits of sex at a relatively young age. And he'd never known a woman quite like Selene. He admired her wit as well as her body. He appreciated her strength. He respected her determination…except at the moment.

Exactly as he'd feared, she'd come to strip him of his control, to melt his emotional armor, to test him. She'd been testing him since she'd walked through the door earlier. And he'd failed miserably. He hadn't been able to mask his jealousy over the thought of her with another man. What she did or who she kept company with shouldn't matter to him. But it did matter, and that could be deadly for both of them.

As she moved toward him with intrinsic grace, he gripped the sofa's arms as if he could anchor himself against his body's sudden ambush. Against the purpose in her brown eyes.

Don't do this to me, Selene….

"I want to do this, Adrien," she said as if he'd voiced his thoughts out loud. "I have to do this."

A burst of fire surged through his body when she leaned over and rubbed her palms down his chest to his abdomen then back up again. "You don't need this tonight," she whispered as she lifted the medallion from his neck and set it beside him, symbolically removing his self-control.

He didn't issue a protest when she slipped the button on his fly and slid his zipper down. Didn't utter a sound when she worked his jeans and briefs down his hips to his thighs. When she straightened to study him, he grew painfully hard right before her eyes.

In business, he was shrewd, unforgiving, never bending to anyone's will. He demanded complete control of his life, at least the aspects that he could control. He didn't welcome any loss of authority. But when Selene knelt before him and lowered her head, he realized what happened next was entirely out of his hands.

She explored him with her tongue from tip to shaft before immersing him completely in the heat of her mouth, causing him to hiss a breath between his clenched teeth. Right now he'd give up what was left of his soul to let her have her way, even though he recognized the risk in that. If he didn't stop her soon, he wouldn't be able to stop her at all.

Selene offered him a reprieve when she came to her feet before him. She took it back when she lifted the gown over her head and tossed it aside, leaving her completely nude.

After she climbed into his lap, her thighs straddling his thighs, she ran her tongue along his bottom lip while brushing her breasts across his chest. "You have two choices, Adrien. You can tell me to leave you alone, and I will, for good. Or you can stop denying what you and I both need and just go with it."

In that moment, what was left of Adrien's resistance splintered. He kissed her hard, kissed her deeply as he lifted her hips with one hand and guided himself inside her with the other, ending months of self-imposed celibacy with one hard upward thrust. It took all his strength not to climax immediately when she surrounded him with tight, wet heat. He braced his palms on her waist, following her movements while keeping his grasp light in order not to bruise her fair skin.

Determined to take her to the limit, he parted his thighs and in turn, parted hers wider, filling her to the hilt. When he broke the kiss and lifted his hips only slightly, he saw awareness pass over her face, witnessed her transformation from genteel lady to unrestrained woman. She kept her gaze connected to his as she rode him hard and fast, as she had in his first fantasy. Now he was at her mercy, and she was taking extreme advantage of that. While she was empowered, he was powerless.

Adrien wanted it to last longer, but his body began to say otherwise, and so did Selene's. He lowered his hands between her legs and stroked her for only a few moments before he felt the pulse of her orgasm that threatened to push him over the edge as well. He cursed his limitations. Cursed his inability to hang on for a while longer. But he didn't curse the climax that charged through him, bringing about a violent shudder that ran the length of his body.

Selene collapsed against him, the sounds of their ragged breathing disrupting the virtually silent night. He threaded his fingers through her hair and rubbed her back until he felt her relax against him. They stayed that way for a time until she lifted her head and touched his face with reverence, looked at him as if he were a man, not a fiend.

"Now that wasn't so difficult, was it?" she asked.

She had no idea how difficult it had been, at least when it came to giving up his control. "You caught me off guard."

"I assumed that was the only way I could get you to cooperate."

"You assumed right."

"And now that my mission is accomplished, I'll leave you to go back to whatever it was you were doing."

Taking Adrien totally by surprise, Selene climbed off his

lap, retrieved the gown and put it back on, then turned and walked back into her room, leaving him with his pants down around his ankles and confusion rolling around in his brain. He'd expected her to request he join her in bed. He'd even secretly hoped she would. Instead, she'd deserted him without requiring more than a fast round of raw sex. And for some reason, that angered him.

In those moments when he'd been joined to her body, he'd felt as if she could absolve him of his sins. But if she discovered what he had done, he could expect only a temporary pardon. Regardless, he wanted more of Selene, and less misery, until she walked away for good.

An hour had passed when Selene felt the bend of the mattress behind her and two solid arms came around her. She was as surprised by Adrien's sudden appearance as she had been by her lack of inhibition on the balcony earlier.

She rolled to face him, separated from his incredible body by only a thin cotton sheet, since she had climbed into bed without clothes. She suspected he didn't have on a stitch, either, and hoped to confirm that soon. "To what do I owe this pleasure?" she asked.

"I didn't realize you were awake."

"Let's just say I'm not used to having a man show up in my bed without any warning."

"Do you want me to leave?"

"I didn't say that." If she did, she wouldn't mean it.

"Good, because I'm not leaving. Not yet." He proved his point by working his way beneath the covers, pulling her closer yet keeping his lower body angled away from her. As she'd suspected, he wasn't wearing a thing, and he smelled so good that Selene nuzzled her nose against his neck. His damp hair brushed against her cheek and her hand automatically traveled there to sift through the soft waves.

Selene had rarely known such euphoria. She delighted in his warmth, his undeniable strength and even his continuing mystery.

He rubbed her back softly, soothingly. "I'll be leaving eventually."

She plied his neck with a series of soft kisses. "I understand. You'd rather spend the night in your own bed."

"I meant I'll be leaving the plantation. I'm going to sell it after it's restored."

That gave her good cause to drag her feet on the renovations, and a reason not to jump into this relationship heart first. It also gave her a sinking feeling in the pit of her stomach. "Where will you be going?"

He curled his hand over her bottom and kneaded it gently. "I'm not sure. Someplace warm if it's winter. Maybe an island."

A deserted island, no doubt. "Are you going to take Ella?"

"No, although I'm sure she'll argue the point. But she won't win."

She suspected not many people experienced the thrill of victory when Adrien was the opposing general.

He slid his thigh between her legs, bringing them into closer contact and making Selene all too aware he was aroused, in turn arousing her. "In the meantime, I want to be your lover until you leave," he said with conviction.

He palmed her breasts lightly, bringing about Selene's sigh. "What about Ella?"

"Three's a crowd."

She laughed even though she wanted to moan. "I meant how is she going to feel about us being together?"

He brushed his knuckles across her belly. "We'll be discreet. And she already has her suspicions."

Surely Selene hadn't been that obvious in her admiration. "Why is that?"

He formed his palm between her thighs. "Because she knows me too well. She knows that I've wanted you since you walked through my door, even though I wanted you gone in the beginning."

"What do you want now, Adrien?" That simple question proved difficult for Selene in light of Adrien's current ministrations, and her fear that she might not like the answer.

"I would think that's obvious," he said as he caressed her without mercy. "I want to be inside you again."

He rolled her away from him and fitted himself against her back before returning his hand between her legs. "No expectations," he said.

"No expectations," she murmured as he lifted her leg over his hip.

"But you can always expect that I'll make you feel..." He eased inside of her. "Very good."

Selene had no doubt that he would exceed those expectations. He already had, and he did again as he rocked against her. Unlike their lovemaking on the veranda, this joining resembled a sensual slow dance, not at all fiery and frenetic, at least not at first. But soon the passion took over on the heels of the sheer electric need that had existed between them since their meeting, setting a feverish tempo until they were both sated and sapped of strength.

After their respiration slowed and their bodies had calmed, Adrien tipped Selene's head back and kissed her. A deep, meaningful kiss that threatened to bring her unsolicited emotions to the surface.

She had to remember to stay grounded, stay guarded. For however long he remained in her life, she would accept his gift of pleasure, yet she would also accept the reality of the situation—he might be the consummate lover, but he was also impossible to hold, and as Ella had so wisely put it, much too easy to love.

First morning light seeping through the window served as Adrien's cue to leave. He wasn't one to hang around for morning-after conversation, but for some reason he couldn't tear himself away. Couldn't stop watching Selene as she slept beside him, one hand curled next to her face, the other resting at her side. Couldn't resist taking another methodical look at her body. Then he would leave.

Careful not to wake her, he clasped the sheet and lowered it to her thighs. He studied her rose-colored nipples before visually tracking the path down her belly to the soft gold shading between her thighs, and went stone hard over the sight. He knew how she tasted all over, how she felt surrounding him when she climaxed, and he wanted to know it all again. And again.

Selene had seeped into his veins like pretty poison, and he needed to get her out of his system. Experience had taught him exactly how to do that. Now he only had to convince her to take the bait, beginning tonight.

Eight

Selene sensed Adrien's presence moments before she looked up to see him standing on the second-floor landing, a striking figure set against the heavenly ceiling. With his dark hair framing his face in soft waves and his translucent blue eyes, he could have fallen away from the band of angels circling overhead.

As she climbed the stairs, her pulse picked up speed in response to his charismatic pull. She hadn't seen him since he'd come to her bed last night, yet he'd never been out of her head for more than a few minutes during the day. She'd replayed their conversation over and over—no expectations, no promises. Only a sexual alliance that would last until her work was done. That bothered her more than she cared to admit, but she couldn't resist him any more than she could will her heart to stop beating, though she could swear it had skipped several beats as she continued her upward climb.

Selene paused at the second stair before the landing, her hand tightly gripping the rail. "I was about to come looking for you. I thought you would like to know that the contractor's set to begin the restoration next Monday, beginning with exterior repairs—"

"What do you have planned for the next two days?"

Apparently he wasn't in the mood to discuss the renovation. Considering the heat in his eyes, he didn't look as if he wanted to talk at all. "Actually, I have nothing scheduled tomorrow or Wednesday. I do have an appointment on Thursday with the woman who's going to restore the furniture, and a crew's coming out to get started on the landscaping."

He leaned forward and grasped the railing, his hands only inches from hers. "Good. I have something I need you to do."

"What would that be?"

"I want you to spend the next forty-eight hours with me, beginning tonight. No phones. No appointments. No interruptions. I only require your trust and undivided attention."

"What will we be doing?" As if she really had to ask. She could already see the mental preview playing out in his mind.

"You know what we'll be doing. And we'll stay in my bedroom where it's cooler, in case you get too hot."

Getting too hot was a given, especially if he planned to hold her captive for hours. "Aren't you afraid we'll get tired of each other?"

"I promise that won't happen."

Selene knew he would make good on that promise. Still, she worried that to take him up on his suggestion could mean certain peril to her emotions. But because her time with Adrien would be limited, she felt the need to make as many memories as possible, as long as she kept a firm hold on her feelings.

In order to avoid any possible interruptions, she had one

last task to complete before she joined him. "I need to call my mother first."

He gave her a wry grin. "To ask her permission?"

"To check in." A call she'd been avoiding for some time now.

"Don't take any longer than necessary." He straightened and subtly brushed his hand over his groin, drawing Selene's attention to the prominent crest outlined against his slacks.

She swallowed hard. "It can wait."

"Are you sure? I wouldn't want to keep you from your family."

"I'm sure." And she was. After all, the phone worked both ways, and her mother hadn't bothered to call her. Right now she had better things to do, interesting places to be, specifically in Adrien's arms. In Adrien's world. At times in Adrien's mind.

Selene took his offered hand without hesitation, more than willing to follow wherever he might lead her. She only hoped that when their time together was over, she wasn't so lost she couldn't find her way back.

Without speaking, Adrien led her into his bedroom that he'd transformed into a seductive lair. Lit candles were scattered about the area, bathing the darkened room in a golden glow. No music played in the background, but the open windows allowed in the sounds of nature's symphony coming from the swamp below.

Adrien pulled Selene down onto a nest of pillows he'd arranged on the floor in the sitting area and removed only their shoes. She noticed a stick of incense burning on the table, emitting an exotic scent that reminded her of warm summer nights in a forest. "That smells really nice."

He reached out and pushed her hair away from her shoulder as he studied her face. "It's a special blend I discovered during my travels. It reportedly has a favorable effect on lovers."

"It's an aphrodisiac, you mean."

"I'd prefer to think of it as an enhancement to an already favorable situation."

She really didn't need any enhancement; she was already experiencing the effects of his smile, the blue fire in his eyes.

"I only have one rule," he said as he began to slip the buttons on her blouse. "No talk of the past. As far as I'm concerned, it doesn't exist as long as we're in this room. Other than that, there are no other rules."

Selene had no concern for the past, only the present when he slid the blouse off her shoulders and removed her bra. He took off his own shirt at his usual leisurely pace while she watched his dynamic chest come into view. Oddly enough, his medallion was missing, which led her to believe that during this respite, he was willing to relinquish his willpower.

Leaving their slacks still intact, he laid her back on the pillows, slid an arm beneath her and settled her against his shoulder. He drew random designs up and down her bare arm with his fingertips as he took her on a journey to the exotic places he'd visited. She watched his mouth as he spoke, admired the way the flickering candlelight played out over his perfect profile, lulled by the sound of his deep voice as he painted a picture with words and, unbeknownst to him, through his thoughts.

Midway through his musings on his travels in Mexico, Selene began to experience a strange tingling in her breasts that took a slow trek downward, followed by a stream of heat. In response, a small sound climbed up her throat and filtered out of her mouth before she could stop it.

Adrien stopped mid-sentence and turned his gaze to her. "You feel it, don't you?"

She highly doubted the incense was responsible for the sudden flash fire of need. It was simply Adrien—a man who was as powerful as any opiate. "I definitely feel something." Her voice sounded winded and raspy.

He tipped her face up and ran the tip of his tongue over her bottom lip. "I'm already hard just thinking about what I want to do to you. What I'm going to do to you."

Selene silently willed him to begin and she got her wish when Adrien sat up and worked her slacks and panties away. She noted a momentary chink in his armor when he stood and fumbled with his fly before removing his slacks and briefs. Now completely nude, he hovered above her and allowed her a long visual exploration, which she gladly took. Because of the limited light, parts of his body had been cast in shadows, but she could see enough to know he was definitely aroused.

He dropped to his knees beside her and leaned to kiss her thoroughly before straightening again. All Selene's senses were heightened—sight, taste, smell and touch. Definitely touch as Adrien sent his hands over her body in a heady excursion. "Tell me what feels good," he whispered as he divined her flesh with a fingertip. "Here?"

"Yes, there," she managed to say on a broken breath when he hit the mark.

He urged her to verbally express her desires as he used both his hands and mouth to bring her to a searing climax, the likes of which she had never known. When her turn came to explore him, he openly talked about what he liked in explicit terms, what drove him wild. And without hesitation, she met every one of his requests with the enthusiasm of a woman caught in the throes of self-discovery.

By the time Adrien eased into her body, Selene felt as if she had traveled to another dimension where nothing existed beyond overwhelming sensation. Where only they existed. As he lifted her hips toward him with his palms and thrust deeply inside her, she experienced another orgasm that seemed to go on for endless moments. Not long after, Adrien released a feral moan as his frame went rigid in her arms. He collapsed against her, his heart pounding against her breasts, his respiration harsh and uneven. Selene breezed her palms down his sculpted back, over his buttocks and up to the damp curls at his nape. She loved the smell of him, the feel of him, even the weight of him.

When he didn't move, she thought maybe he'd fallen asleep until he muttered, "I'm wasted," in her ear.

Selene wasn't wasted at all. In fact, she had already begun to feel the stirrings of more need. Framing his jaws in her palms, she lifted his head and forced him to look at her. "Please don't tell me we're through for the night."

His grin lit up his eyes—and Selene's heart. "I said I'm wasted, not dead. I predict I'll recover quickly."

Adrien's prediction proved to be correct as they again made love two more times during the night. Shortly before dawn, they fell asleep curled together on the pillows and Selene awoke to find him staring at her.

"Good morning," she said as she stretched her arms above her head. "What time is it?"

"Does it matter?"

She supposed it really didn't. After all, she had nothing better to do than stay in his arms. She could think of nothing better to do. "I'm just used to being up by now."

"I'm already up."

Her gaze immediately tracked downward to discover proof of that. "Well, you can always count on three things. Death, taxes and a man's morning erection."

Adrien laughed then, a deep throaty laugh that lifted Selene's spirits even more. "Why, sir, I didn't realize you had a sense of humor," she said.

He tugged her against him. "And I didn't realize the extent of your charms."

As far as Selene was concerned, he had a surplus of charm that matched his monetary worth. "Could I charm you into some more of what we had last night?"

"Do you really have to ask?"

As it turned out, she didn't.

In the following hours, time seemed to suspend as Adrien kept Selene captive in an erotic haze. At noon, he led her outside onto the veranda, backing her up against the alcove surrounding the doors where anyone could come upon them, their bodies soon slick from the heat of the blazing sun and their unrestrained lovemaking. Selene had never felt so liberated, nor had she realized that taking such a risk could be such a turn-on. But Adrien knew, just like he knew exactly how and when to bring her to a glorious climax while he was seated deep within her body.

Though they left the room only when necessary, they didn't devote every moment to lovemaking. Adrien insisted on attending to her every need, including bringing them food and drink. He seemed more open, more relaxed than before as they talked about many things, including their preference for Southern authors and their disdain for politics. When she asked about his parents, he only said they were both gone, and left it at that. His apparent distress, which he unsuccessfully tried to hide, prevented Selene from asking for details. In accordance with his insistence they forget the past, he didn't mention her ex-husband, and she didn't inquire about the woman who'd once been in his life. But when she told him the ill-fated lovers' story, stressing her sadness over Grace's death and Zeke wasting away due to grief, she knew he could relate.

Several times she'd considered telling him about her abilities, but she'd worried he might not understand. That he might even call an end to their interlude before she was ready. Eventually she would tell him, when she felt the time was right.

At sundown, he prodded her to try his eighty-year-old scotch and when she wrinkled her nose and coughed, he laughed. She loved hearing his laughter, loved that he seemed to be transforming right before her eyes though he still retained the mystery that had drawn her from the beginning. They dined in bed and showered together in Adrien's well-appointed bathroom. Even that had been an experience Selene would never forget, as Adrien made love to her in ways she'd never dreamed possible, always careful to concentrate on her pleasure, never once causing her pain. And on the second day, they did more of the same—more touches, more talk, more unbelievable lovemaking.

Selene had never had such control of her own pleasure and, at times, of Adrien. She'd learned how to taunt him just so she could hear him plead with her in his low, drugging voice. She delighted in her newfound power as well as her recently discovered freedom. She reveled in what Adrien had shown her—that she was a desirable woman who could bring a man to his knees with only a touch.

By the time they reached the end of their escape from reality, Selene had done things she'd never considered doing before, had talked about things she'd never considered discussing, and had totally fallen for Adrien. She felt as if in many ways they were not only connected by their minds but also by their souls. Yet she still didn't completely understand the source of his sorrow even though he'd seemed to let go of that during the past two days. But when she awoke in the middle of the night to find him staring out the window, she realized he'd only had a temporary reprieve from his torment. She did all she could think to do—ask him to make love to her one final time, which he did, with a surprising tenderness forever imprinted in her memories.

And before she drifted off once more in his arms, Selene accepted that he would forever occupy a special place in her heart, and intended or not, he had won her love.

On Thursday morning, Selene awoke to find Adrien gone, and she felt completely bereft, as if she'd lost a lifelong friend, a cherished lover. She gave herself a good mental scolding for doing exactly what she'd vowed to avoid—falling in love with him. But she didn't know how to quell the feelings that continued to bubble up to the surface. How to stop thinking about him for more than a few minutes during the day even though she hadn't seen him since the night before. Unfortunately, she had no choice but to return to the real world.

After meeting with the furniture restorer at half-past noon, Selene gathered up a few fabric samples to use as an excuse to see Adrien.

She arrived at his office to find the door partially ajar and stepped inside, where Adrien paced the area behind his desk, clutching a cordless phone tightly in his grasp. "I said just do it, dammit. You're being paid well for your services."

After he slammed the phone down on the charger, Selene considered backing out quietly until his gaze shot to hers and his anger seemed to diminish.

"I've obviously caught you at a bad time," she said as she hugged the samples to her breasts. "I'll come back later."

He ran a fast hand through his hair before bracing his palms on the back of his chair. "You don't have to leave. I could use a distraction right now."

She took a few steps forward and held up the pieces of fabric. "For the main parlor downstairs, do you like the red-and-gold pinstripe or the green brocade?"

He rubbed his chin, sat down in his chair and smiled. "Tell you what. Take off your clothes and wrap up in them, one at a time, and I'll tell you which one I prefer."

She feigned a frown. "You're insatiable."

"I could say the same about you."

He could, and he would be correct. Right now she wanted to climb into his lap as she had on the veranda when she'd set their lovemaking into full swing. Climb all over him, as a matter of fact. "Now back to business. Which one do you like?"

He sat and leaned back in his chair. "You choose. I'm sure you have a better eye for color than I do."

She definitely had an eye for gorgeous men, and her eye was on the one sitting before her, with his wavy rogue's hair and his irrefutable sensual aura. "All right, if I must. Or I can consult with Ella when she returns. Any idea when that might be?"

"On Saturday. I told her to stay longer, but she refused. She claims she's wearing out her welcome."

As much as Selene wanted to see Ella, she couldn't prevent the nip of disappointment that their alone time had come to an end. But hopefully not their lovemaking. "I'm looking forward to seeing her."

He pushed back his chair, stood and braced his palms on the desk. "I'm not. I planned to make love to you in every room in this house. Of course, we could manage that in the next two days."

And that would quite possibly be the death of Selene. "We'll see, but right now I have something I'd like for you to do."

He presented *that* look, the one that said he meant business. Sensual business. "Climb up on my desk and I'll take care of it."

And she knew exactly how he would take care of it

through the mental signals he sent out that her brain picked up like a high-frequency scanner. "This isn't about sex, Adrien. I want to take a walk around the place as soon as it cools off a bit." She definitely needed to cool off, too. "I want you to come with me."

"Any particular reason why?"

"Mr. Gutherie told me he used to come here during the summers and play in a tree house. I want to see if it's still there."

"It is," he said. "In a pecan grove."

"You've seen it?"

The sparkle in his eyes gave way to recognizable regret "Yeah. I've explored most of the acreage surrounding the house."

"That must have taken quite a while."

"I had nothing better to do at the time."

She wanted desperately to ask him why he was so sad, but instead of coming right out and posing the query, she decided to take an indirect route. "Before I forget, I need to know what you want me to do about the guest room across from yours. Ella told me you didn't want it disturbed, but if you're worried about valuables, I can help you move them to a safe place while the redecorating is in progress."

Now he looked annoyed. "I want the room to stay as it is."

"For how long?"

"Until I say otherwise. Is that understood?"

He had all but confirmed that the clue to his distress could be found in that room. But would she risk trying to find out? Maybe after Ella's return she would consider it. Right now, she simply needed to lighten the mood. "Why, yes sir, I understand you completely. I might be insatiable, but I am certainly not deaf. Or stupid."

Selene could tell he didn't want to let go of the anger,

but he lost the battle and smiled. "No, you're definitely not stupid."

She pointed behind her. "Now that I know my intelligence is not in question, I'll go and let you get back to business. I'll meet you downstairs on the front porch at around six, if that works for you."

He rounded the desk and approached her with his usual slow, stalking gait. "Have you ever made love up against a tree, Selene?"

"I've never even considered it." She was now.

He slid his arms around her waist and pulled her to him. "Don't underestimate the power of nature. Don't underestimate my power."

That power was palpable, particularly when he kissed her. She was veritable putty in his arms, available for him to shape however he saw fit. And right then she understood she was hurling at breakneck speed straight into trouble.

With Adrien at her side, Selene walked backward through the field, studying the plantation now washed in the glow of the setting sun, trying to visualize what it would look like once the black columns had been painted white. *"Maison de Soleil.* The House of Sunshine," she said as she turned to face forward and plucked a lone dandelion from the grass. "We definitely need to rename the house after it's restored."

When Adrien didn't immediately respond, she tapped him on his shoulder. "Don't you agree?"

He glanced at her as they continued walking. "With what?"

"That we should rename the plantation *Maison de Soleil,* what it was called before."

"Before what?"

Obviously his thoughts had left for parts unknown.

"Before Grace passed away. Maybe we should ask Zeke, the former owner, his opinion. Jeb Gutherie told me his grandmother used to talk to him after he died, although Jeb claims Zeke has gone on to the great unknown."

That earned her a sour look from Adrien. "I don't believe people can commune with the dead," he said. "I don't believe in ghosts or voodoo or the sight."

Of course he wouldn't, Selene thought. He was a businessman. Pragmatic to a fault. And probably not yet ready to accept her "gift." "Then you don't believe that some things can't be explained?"

"No, I don't." He sounded insulted that she'd even asked.

"What about destiny?"

"We create our own destinies. We're responsible for our actions and our choices."

Selene plucked the petals from the flower, silently chanting, *Tell him, or tell him not.* She reached the last petal and ended with *Tell him not.* Maybe later. Much later. Or never.

"It's over there," he said, pointing to a grove of large pecan trees bordering the open field.

Selene quickened her pace when she caught sight of the log platform braced by two heavy limbs. She couldn't believe the tree house had survived all these years. She also couldn't quite fathom why she had the urge to run to it and climb, but she did exactly that. She'd barely gotten one foot up onto one low-hanging branch when Adrien said, "Don't do it, Selene."

She chose to ignore him and hoisted herself up onto the larger limb. "I want to do it. I wasn't allowed to climb when I was a child."

"Get down now."

With one foot planted on the log platform, ready to take the final step, she regarded him over her shoulder. "Why? It looks sturdy enough."

He strode to the tree and gave her a harsh stare. "Looks can be deceptive. It's old and probably rotted. You could fall and break something."

She appreciated his concern on one level, but resented that he believed she was incapable of taking care of herself on another. "I'm just going to test it with my foot. I won't put all my weight on it yet."

Before she could make her next move, she felt a solid grip on her ankle. "I said get down. Now."

Although he sounded livid, Selene noted a hint of real fear in his tone. "If you're that worried, okay."

As she began to climb down, her foot slipped and so did her grasp on the limb. Before she tumbled out of the tree, Adrien was there, gathering her into his arms. He immediately set her on her feet and backed away from her. "I told you not to do it, dammit."

Selene braced her hands on her hips. "I wasn't that far from the ground, Adrien. If I had fallen, I probably would have injured only my pride."

"Or you could have broken your neck, and God knows you wouldn't want to deal with that."

He spun away from her and headed toward the house. Selene had a hard time keeping up with him and an even more difficult time understanding why he was so angry. She managed to clutch his arm but he shook off her grasp and kept walking.

"What is wrong with you?" she said through her ragged respiration.

He stopped dead and faced her. "There's not a damn thing wrong with me. But you're too stubborn."

Her mouth dropped open a few seconds before she momentarily clamped it closed. "And you're being hypocritical, he who has jumped from planes and dived off of cliffs."

"That was a long time ago. The risk isn't worth it. I learned that the hard way."

Again he tried to move on but this time she wouldn't let him. She sprinted until she was in front of him and put up both her hands to stop his progress. "Don't walk away from me, Adrien. Not until you explain what this is all about."

"Your safety."

She held out her arms and slowly turned around. "See? I'm still in one piece."

"I don't have the energy or desire to deal with your carelessness."

"I'm not asking you to deal with anything. I'm a big girl and quite capable of taking care of myself."

A few brief images filtered into Selene's mind—a smiling young woman, and that same woman in a free fall, her eyes filled with terror, before everything faded to black.

Adrien turned away again and managed a few steps until Selene said, "Does this have something to do with Chloe?" He faced her again with a menacing look that made her shrink back. Made her want to run for the cover of the trees.

"Has Ella been talking to you?" he said, his tone as irate as his expression.

Selene folded her arms across her middle. "No, she hasn't. But I know Chloe existed. I know she's someone you cared about. Maybe even someone you loved."

He fisted his hands at his sides. "You don't know a damn thing about me. And you're better off not knowing."

With that, he turned and headed back for the house and, this time, Selene let him go. She was no closer to having the answers she craved. No closer to understanding his relationship with Chloe. But she did understand the depth of his grief and that Chloe had indeed been an important part of his life. She also knew something had happened to her. Something horrible, and that loss was still eating away at Adrien.

Selene vowed to find out all the facts eventually, hopefully not before it was too late to save him from a future of utter despair.

Adrien had no idea how she'd found out about Chloe. He only knew that she was coming too close to the truth.

Overcome with rage, he cleared his desk with one sweep of his arm before he paced the room, restless with turmoil and confusion. He despised indecision and weakness, almost as much as he'd despised himself at the moment.

He'd mistakenly believed that by spending so much time with Selene, he would discover something about her he didn't like. Something that would make it easy for him to let her go. Instead, he'd fallen victim to his own machinations. She wasn't out of his system at all. He was consumed by her.

In her presence, he'd begun to forget his failings, and that was something he couldn't allow himself to do. Forgetting would be the true mark of a man who was devoid of conscience, and totally beyond salvation. He hadn't arrived at that place. At least not yet.

He also recognized that Selene didn't deserve the brunt of his anger. She deserved a man who was whole. A man without a history of irreparable mistakes. A man who could love her the way she should be loved.

Yet in those hours he'd spent with her, at times he'd believed he could be that man. She'd given him hope that maybe he could move beyond what had been to what might be. Until the memories had been resurrected that afternoon, reminding him of the impossible.

He knew of only one way to assure her imminent

rejection—by telling her the truth. An extreme measure, and a last resort.

In the meantime, he would spend one last evening pretending he was the man she believed him to be—before he returned to damnation.

rejection. She told me her hu... ...An extremely pleasant
...and a handsome ... ...
...
...

Nine

After spending the night restless and alone, Selene decided to return to the near-barren nursery the following morning. She sat in the rocking chair and set it in motion with her heel, staring at the cradle while thinking about poor Grace, who'd never had the chance to hold her baby. Who'd been torn from her husband's life all too soon, sending him spiraling into a state of grief from which he'd never emerged. That kind of devastating loss was totally foreign to Selene. Of course, several of her relatives had succumbed to old age. Otherwise, she'd not suffered too much loss, with the exception of her marriage—a marriage that had been hopeless from the beginning. At least she hadn't made the fatal mistake of getting pregnant, although at times she'd wondered if a child could have alleviated some of the loneliness. Yet bringing a baby into a world with two parents who didn't really love each other would have been cruel.

Selene sighed and nudged the cradle that was as empty as she felt at the moment. Every instinct told her to leave Adrien alone, maybe even to leave this place. But something was keeping her here. An unknown force, or fate. Or perhaps it was simply her hope that Adrien might eventually love her, too.

"Wishful thinking, Selene?"

Selene shifted around to find him leaning against the doorjamb wearing his standard white shirt and black slacks, as if he'd recently walked out of a corporate meeting. She couldn't stop her spirits from soaring or her heart's quickening.

She came to her feet and opted for business talk to mask her continuing hurt over his behavior. "I was thinking maybe this would make a nice family room. It could be more modern than the rest of the house, and that might provide a good selling point when you put it on the market."

He continued to study her for a long moment before he said, "I'm sorry."

Selene hadn't expected that at all. "Apology accepted."

He rubbed a hand over his nape and studied the floor in very un-Adrien-like fashion. "I know it's a lot to ask, but I would like to make it up to you tonight."

Another surprise. "How do you propose to do that?"

"By having dinner with you. A real dinner that you don't have to prepare."

A real date? That was probably too much to ask, Selene decided. "Will we be dining out?"

He finally lifted his gaze to her. "No. I've arranged for the meal to be brought in."

Her disappointment filtered out on a long sigh. "It wouldn't hurt you to get out of the house now and then."

He slid his hands into his pockets. "I have my reasons for not wanting to leave tonight."

She suspected that might have to do with what he planned as an after-dinner treat. But she wasn't going to go there, not until she had some answers.

Selene strolled toward him but kept a safe distance. "What time?"

"Seven."

"Fine. I guess I'll see you then."

When she brushed past him, he caught her hand and tugged her into his arms. She expected a kiss, but what she got was an embrace. He simply held her for a long moment, his palms pressed against her back and his cheek resting against her cheek. When he kissed her forehead, Selene asked, "What was that for?"

"For being you." She noted a warmth in his eyes that she'd never seen before, as if his emotional fortress had dissolved, at least for the time being.

Ironically, in all the years she'd been with Richard, not once had he ever remotely made her feel as special as she did with Adrien. "Thank you," she said. "I like you, too." In truth, she loved him. All his mystery, his hidden humanity, the man she knew resided beneath the steely exterior. A man so wrought with pain that he couldn't get past it to save his life.

His expression turned somber. "Your respect means a lot to me, Selene. More than you know."

But she did know. Her intuition was screaming that he cared about her. That he could love her, too, in the future. But not unless he finally unveiled the foundation of his tragic past.

And when he let her go and walked away, she understood they were quickly approaching the proverbial point of no return. If she couldn't get him to come clean tonight, then she would have to decide whether to fight or accept defeat. Accept that she wasn't "the one," as Ella had predicted.

But as long as she was with him, she still had hope that maybe, just maybe, he was an important part of her destiny.

Wearing the black satin dress she'd purchased that day, her hair done up in a neat twist, Selene descended the stairs as fast as her strappy heels would let her. She'd waited until five minutes after the hour in order to be fashionably late, and to let Adrien know she wasn't completely under his command. As she reached the dining room, she pulled up short when she spotted a lanky gray-haired stranger wearing a black tuxedo standing outside the opening.

"Good evening, miss," he said. "I'm Mr. Renaldo, your waiter for the evening. Right this way."

Speechless, Selene took his offered arm and allowed him to escort her into the dining room. When she entered, she found Adrien standing by the table dressed in a black silk jacket and slacks and a crisp white shirt. She immediately noticed their place settings had been set side by side, not at opposite ends of the table. The waiter pulled back Selene's chair and, after she was seated, draped a pink cloth napkin in her lap.

When the man disappeared into the kitchen and Adrien was settled in beside her, Selene asked, "Where did he come from?"

"Atlanta. He accompanied the chef from Chez Gaston. I thought you might miss your hometown, and this was a way to bring it to you."

"I know the place well, and I can't believe they drove all the way here on a Friday night." She couldn't believe Adrien had been so thoughtful.

"I had them flown in by private jet."

Unbelievable. "That seems like quite a bit of expense.

I really had no problem heating up one of the dinners Ella made for us."

Adrien draped an arm over the back of her chair. "Do you have something against having a top-rate meal?"

No, but Selene did have somewhat of an aversion to money. She also surmised that the extent of Adrien's wealth went beyond her expectations. Nothing she hadn't known all of her life, another aspect she'd been trying to escape. Now here she sat, with a man who had enough funds to bring in his own preeminent chef and waiter. And enough emotional baggage to fill an airport. "I'm sorry. I didn't mean to sound ungrateful. I appreciate it very much."

His eyes took on that smoky hue she found so hard to resist. "You'll definitely appreciate everything I have planned tonight."

Adrien unabashedly studied her breasts unencumbered beneath the black silk and a sudden fantasy-flash called out from his mind and landed in hers.

He never arranged for a private dining room in an exclusive restaurant, then touched you beneath the table until you wanted it right then, right there….

Surely he wasn't considering… Oh, but he was, that much Selene knew. And just thinking about it sent a hot blush rushing to her cheeks. At this rate, she was going to have a difficult time maintaining her resolve to avoid any more intimacy until she had answers.

He circled his fingertips round and round her bare shoulder. "I like this dress," he said. "But I would have preferred something a little lower cut."

She touched the high collar that now felt like a noose around her neck. "I wanted to wear something special, but I didn't have anything appropriate so I had to go into town to buy it. Unfortunately, this was the best I could do on such short notice. But the lady at the boutique was very helpful and accommodating."

"I certainly plan to be accommodating."

Selene had no doubt about that. She also had little doubt that the meal would be unforgettable when Mr. Renaldo brought in the shrimp-and-scallop appetizer. As soon as he left, Adrien laid his hand on Selene's knee beneath the napkin. As each course was served, his palm inched higher, and her pulse rose in anticipation. He was definitely teasing her. And it was working very well.

By the time the entrée arrived, she wasn't certain she could choke down another bite even though her dinner companion had yet to do anything questionable other than stroke his thumb along the inside of her leg.

Adrien managed to consume all the food, including the strawberry crepes that Selene waved away. She did accept the offer of a second glass of wine though Adrien hadn't finished half of his first.

After Mr. Renaldo cleared the final plate and retreated into the kitchen, Adrien leaned over and whispered, "You know, he's totally oblivious. I could—"

She slapped her palm on his hand before he hit the intended target. "But he's not blind, and if you do what I think you're going to do, I promise he'll know."

Adrien took her hand and held it to his lips for a kiss. "I was only wondering if you're wearing anything underneath this dress."

"Yes, I am." A barely-there scrap of black silk.

Before the discussion could continue, the waiter re-entered the room with the man who introduced himself as Chef Stephan Aucoin, a portly gentleman who looked as if he routinely consumed most of the food he prepared.

Adrien pushed away from the table and came to his feet. "Gentlemen, as always, you did an excellent job."

The chef executed a little bow. "Our pleasure, Mr. Morrell." He turned his attention to Selene. "Ms. Winston, you barely ate. Did you not find the food to your liking?"

"She doesn't eat well when she's hot," Adrien said, followed by a wry grin aimed at her.

"It's the summer weather," Selene quickly added. If she could reach Adrien's foot, she'd stomp it.

"Then we will have to return when the weather's cooler," Renaldo said.

Unbeknownst to them, she would probably be gone before the weather turned cooler.

Adrien checked his watch and rounded the table. "Your car's waiting to take you back to the airport." He reached inside his jacket, withdrew an envelope and handed it to the chef. "I'll see you out."

After Adrien escorted the men out of the room, Selene slumped down in her chair and fanned her face, surprised that she'd gotten through the evening without fainting. She was high on adrenaline and definitely warm, but not because of the elements. She grew warmer still when Adrien strolled into the dining room, hands in his pockets and a sultry look on his face.

Selene stood and pushed her chair beneath the table, using it for support. "She doesn't eat when she's hot? I cannot believe you said that."

He had the nerve to grin. "You are hot, aren't you?"

She was, and damn him, he knew it. "I'm cooling off now."

He stalked toward her and before she could move out of his path, he had her securely in his arms. After lifting the back of her dress, he ran his palm over her bottom. "I want these off of you."

She wrested out of his arms and stepped back, earning Adrien's frown. "First, we need to talk."

"About what?"

"About our secrets. Yours and mine."

He narrowed his eyes. "Everyone should be entitled to their secrets, Selene. I don't need your revelations."

Folding her arms beneath her breasts, she strolled to the opposite side of the room, putting the table between them. "Well, I'm going to make one. And you're going to listen."

He pulled back a chair and dropped down into it. "Go ahead and confess if it makes you feel better. But don't expect me to do the same."

Oh, but she did, especially after she said what should have been said a while ago. She drew in a cleansing breath and remained standing, her hands braced on the back of a chair. "When I was a little girl, I learned I had this innate ability to tap into other people's thoughts. I also learned it wasn't always a good thing, knowing what other people thought about you. Knowing what you were going to get on your birthday and Christmas. I taught myself how to block it out."

She waited for his response, but when he just sat there, looking cynical, she continued. "After my ex-husband started staying out well into the night with the excuse he was working, I decided to utilize my *gift* for the first time in years. Imagine my surprise when I discovered while he was in bed with me, he was fantasizing about a mutual friend. I called him on it, he admitted to the affair. End of story and end of marriage."

He shifted slightly in the chair. "I told you, I don't believe in that kind of thing."

In other words, he didn't believe her, but he would. "The moment I stepped into this house, your thoughts began to come to me. I didn't invite them, but they were too strong to block."

He pushed back from the table and stood up. "This is ridiculous."

"Is it?" Selene tightened her grip on the chair. "When I came to you on the veranda the first time we made love, I knew you'd fantasized about it because I'd been privy to those fantasies."

He seemed to mull it over for a minute before the skepticism returned to his expression. "Is there a point to all this?"

"Yes, there is." She moved around the table and stood only a few feet from him. "I've picked up other images from you. Images about the woman named Chloe. In fact, you're the one who told me her name inadvertently."

He shoved one chair and knocked it over. "I don't have to listen to this."

"Yes, you do, because I know something happened to her. And whatever it is, it's eating away at you like acid."

Without saying a word, he stormed out of the room and into the vestibule, Selene close on his heels.

"Stop and listen to me, Adrien," she demanded before he managed the first stair.

He faced her again, his expression heralding a bitter anger. "Why should I?"

"Because I've given you my trust from the beginning. Because I trusted you enough to tell you something only one other living soul knows. And now I'm asking you to trust me enough to tell me about her."

"If you really have this ability to read minds, you already know the whole sordid story."

She took another step toward him. "I don't know everything because you've managed to keep those thoughts from me. And maybe I've made a subconscious effort not to know because I was afraid you've done something terrible."

"You would be right about that."

She moved to the bottom of the staircase within his reach, determined to prod him until she had all the answers. "Then you owe it to me to tell me the truth. I want to know about Chloe. What happened to her. What it was about her that made you love her so much that you completely bowed out of life when she was gone."

He collapsed onto the second stair and lowered his head into his hands. When he looked up, his eyes reflected a sorrow so deep, it took Selene's breath.

Adrien's mind became an open floodgate then, sending a barrage of images into Selene's mind in rapid-fire succession. A young, dark-haired, blue-eyed woman climbing, then reaching out for a hand, unable to hold on. Falling, her body twisting, slamming against the wall of rock before dangling lifeless from a tether. The same woman who'd come to Selene in her dreams.

When the visions began to fade, Selene dropped down beside Adrien on the stair. "She fell."

He studied her with weary eyes. "She wasn't an experienced climber. She shouldn't have gone with me, but she begged me to go. And I didn't refuse her. I never could."

"You must have loved her very much."

"As much as anyone could love a sister."

Selene's shock came out in a slight gasp. "Sister?"

He swiped a hand over his forehead. "Yeah. She was born when I was twelve to my mother and my bastard of a stepfather. Chloe was the only good thing that came out of that sham of a marriage." He released a caustic laugh. "Ironically, Giles had control of the inheritance, and he willed it all to me. He made me administrator of Chloe's trust. Needless to say, that didn't set too well with my mother or her sorry husband who had designs on her money. Neither did the fact that Chloe remained in touch with me after I left home at sixteen to live with Giles. And now they blame me for the accident, and as bad as I hate to admit it, that blame is justified."

Selene draped an arm around his shoulder. "It's not your fault. You said yourself it was an accident."

He leaned forward, bent elbows resting on his knees, and streaked both hands over his face. "I don't want to talk about this anymore."

Instinct told Selene several pieces of the puzzle were still missing. But since he looked as if he'd been put through the wringer, she decided she'd learned enough for now. "I'm sorry, Adrien. But I'm not sorry you finally told me. I just wanted to take some of this burden away from you."

His blue eyes held a cast of confusion. "Why, Selene?"

"Because I care about you. When we're together, I'm happier than I've been in years. When we're apart, I feel like a part of me is missing. And I know you told me no expectations, no promises, but I can't help the way I feel."

He turned toward her and framed her face in his palms. "I don't deserve your compassion. I don't deserve spending even another minute with you. But God help me, I can't stay away from you."

His kiss was demanding and desperate, his touch deliberate as he leaned her back and sent his hands down her body to lift her dress. When he slid her panties away, she didn't bother to protest because she knew it would be futile—she wanted this as much as he did. When he undid his fly and nudged her legs apart, she saw no point in telling him they might be more comfortable in bed, because comfort wasn't his immediate concern. He wasn't seeking the unconventional, either; he needed a connection. Needed the one thing that had provided solace from the pain he had endured, and she was more than willing to provide that comfort.

He levered his knee on the stair and thrust inside her,

sending a slow-moving flame flowing throughout Selene's body. When he buried his face in the bend of her neck, she looked up at the cherubs soaring above them in the blissful blue sky. A fitting scene in so many ways since Adrien's mastery was pure paradise. But his torment contrasted with the peaceful depiction.

She closed her eyes and let the sensations take over, allowed Adrien to take the lead as he guided her back to the place where no painful past existed, only pleasure. As always, her body responded to his touch and her mind reached out to share in his physical gratification, as well as his emotional turmoil.

After a time, his frame went rigid and, following a long shudder, he whispered, "Don't leave me, Selene."

She assumed he meant only tonight, though she didn't want to leave him now, or ever for that matter. She was unmistakably connected to him, heart and soul. Destiny *had* played a part in their meeting, and now that she knew the truth, knew that he was simply a wounded man, not a murderer, Selene didn't intend to ignore it.

She couldn't move her arms or legs. Couldn't utter a word or a scream. Couldn't pull away the fingers tightening around her throat. In a matter of minutes, she would die at the hand of some unknown assailant. When she saw the flash of a gold medallion, she realized he wasn't a stranger after all.

Selene bolted upright, gasping for air and shaking uncontrollably. Her gaze zipped to the now-empty space once occupied by Adrien, her mind running rampant with the unspeakable possibilities. Had she given her heart to a murdering demon, not a fallen angel?

Adrien had said he was administrator of Chloe's trust, but would he stage an accident to claim her inheritance all because of greed? She refused to believe that her instincts about him had failed her completely, even as the disturbing images continued to play out in her mind while she dressed quickly in the clothes she'd so easily discarded the night before. But she didn't have time to make her escape before he came out of the bathroom wearing only a low-slung towel around his hips and a slight smile.

He leaned one shoulder against the wall and folded his arms across his bare chest. "Where are you going?"

Caught between walking into his arms and running away, Selene backed toward the door. "I thought I should get dressed before Ella comes home."

"She's already here."

That relieved Selene somewhat in case her concerns turned out to have merit—he'd murdered his own flesh and blood. "Good. I look forward to seeing how her trip went." And to demand answers. Beg for them if she had to.

When Adrien pushed off the wall, Selene backed up another step. "What's wrong, Selene?" he asked.

She didn't dare tell him about her visions. Didn't dare give her suspicions away. "Nothing's wrong. I'm just afraid Ella will catch me in your bedroom."

He released a low laugh. "As far as I'm concerned, she'll have to get used to it. I expect you to be in my bed from now on."

Last night, she would have given anything to hear him say that. But now, she didn't know what to think. "I'll see you later." Provided she wasn't forced to get out while she still could.

Without affording him another glance, Selene rushed into the hall bathroom and locked the door. She made quick work of her morning routine and when she hurried into her bedroom to dress, she noticed the message display flashing on her cell phone. One of her parents had tried to contact her only an hour ago, and although she was tempted to put off returning the call, she felt the need to make the connection with her family.

After collapsing onto the edge of the bed, she depressed the speed-dial number and her father immediately answered in his Southern-sophisticate tone.

"Hi, Dad. It's Selene. Sorry I missed your call."

"You're missing more than that, pumpkin. Your sister is in labor. She insisted I inform you immediately."

Hannah had been known for her bad timing, but perhaps in this instance, she'd displayed good timing. An excuse for Selene to leave. But would she have any peace at all if she didn't have the truth about Adrien before she returned home? No. "Have they said how long before the baby's born?"

"Last report from your mother, who by the way is still not speaking to you, the midwife said it could be several hours. Perhaps even tomorrow."

Not a surprise that her mother was still angry, something Selene would have to deal with later. "Then she's still determined to have the baby at home?"

"Yes, she is, although I have no idea why when hospitals and pain relievers are readily available in this day and time. Are you still in godforsaken Louisiana?"

Obviously Hannah had filled him in, which was okay since it saved Selene from explaining, although more questions were in the offing. "Yes, I'm still here." At least for now. "Tell Hannah good luck, and I'll be there as soon as I'm able."

As soon as she made the effort to find some answers. The decision to stay in Georgia for good, or return to Louisiana to be with Adrien, rested on what she discovered. The best place to begin was with the woman downstairs. And Selene had no time to waste.

* * *

"Welcome back, Ella."

Seated at a small desk in the kitchen, Ella glanced up from a stack of mail she'd been sorting. "Hello to you, too, Selene. I was beginning to think you'd left, considering it's almost noon and I hadn't seen you yet."

"Actually, I do have to leave for a couple of days. My sister's having her baby and I want to be there. But first, I need your help."

Ella stared at Selene over her half glasses. "I can hold down the fort while you're gone for a few days. Just let me know what I need to do."

Grabbing a nearby chair, Selene pulled it close to Ella. "This doesn't have anything to do with the restoration. It has to do with Adrien. I need to know what really happened to Chloe."

Ella turned back to the envelopes. "I've told you, I can't speak about that. I've given Adrien my word."

She touched Ella's arm to regain her attention. "Look, I know she suffered a fall while they were climbing and she died. Adrien told me that much. But I'm worried about what he's not telling me. I need to know if he's responsible for her death. If in fact it really was an accident."

"Why is this so important to you?"

"Because I care about Adrien. If he's done something horrible, I have to know."

Ella studied her a long moment. "You've fallen in love with him, haven't you?"

Denial seemed to be the best course, but Selene doubted she could pull it off. "I want to believe that it was only an accident. But my instincts are telling me there's more to it than that." Instincts she could no longer ignore.

"It *was* an accident, but that's only part of the story."

She sent Ella a pleading look. "Then tell me everything. Please."

Without commenting further, Ella pulled a key from a cubbyhole in the shelf above the desk, then slid it toward Selene. "In the room across from his. Second drawer in the nightstand. You'll find the answers there."

Selene went to her feet and laid a palm on Ella's shoulder. "Thank you," she said before she rushed out of the kitchen.

She hurried up the staircase, but the uncertainty over what she might discover in the drawer slowed her steps as she reached the dim hallway. When she noticed Adrien's door ajar, she assumed he had gone to his office. She *prayed* he had gone to his office.

While the bronze demon looked on with his treacherous eyes and frightening sneer, Selene fumbled with the key, dropping it twice before finally tripping the lock. She opened the door, expecting to find a room that housed treasured memories of Chloe. She found no keepsakes, no pictures, nothing that would indicate a young woman had resided there at all. Instead, she discovered a narrow hospital bed set lengthwise against one window, the nightstand Ella had mentioned beside it. And leaning against the wall at the end of that bed, a folded wheelchair.

Seeing the room only served to bring about more questions, not answers. She speculated that Chloe hadn't died in the accident and instead suffered some sort of paralysis. In order to confirm that fact, Selene walked to the nightstand and slid open the drawer to find several pieces of paper. Sketches, she realized when she lifted them from the bottom of the drawer, took at seat on the wooden floor and laid them on her crossed legs. Watercolor depictions of butterflies and trees, winged birds taking flight, including a little girl with dark curls running across what appeared to be the plantation's front lawn, with the house—painted all yellow—serving as a backdrop. But the saddest one of all featured a young woman, sitting profile in a wheelchair, her face covering her hands—the tragic portrayal of what Chloe had become. And below that, Selene came upon a note written in precise script.

Dear Adrien,
    I hate that I've become such a burden for you and Ella. But I hate leaving you both even more. Please don't make me do this. I'm not that strong.
        Forgive me,
        Chloe

More questions filtered into Selene's mind. Inconceivable questions. What had Adrien wanted his sister to do, and why was she asking his forgiveness? Had he tried to convince her that dying was the only way out, and she'd refused? Had he in turn taken her life to release her from her misery, or himself from the burden?

Needing more clues, Selene stood and opened the top drawer, the drawings and note still clutched in one hand. She found myriad medical supplies, including syringes and bottles, but the item in the corner drew all her attention. She lifted the photo from the drawer, a snapshot of Adrien and Chloe dressed in winter gear, snowcapped mountains surrounding them, their heads tipped together and energetic smiles on their faces. One thing Selene couldn't deny—this brother and sister loved each other very much. Yet something had gone terribly wrong....

"What in the hell are you doing in here, Selene?"

Ten

Selene nearly dropped everything when she turned to find
Adrien standing in the open doorway, fury flashing in his
blue eyes. She held up the pictures and note. "I was looking
for these."

His gaze shot to the papers. "What did you expect to find?"

"Answers. I now know that Chloe lived through the
accident, and that she ended up in a wheelchair. I still don't
know what happened after that, and I need to know." She
prepared to ask the question weighing heaviest on her
mind, despite the possible fallout. "Did you have something to do with her death?"

If he was at all shocked that she'd asked, he didn't
show it. "Yes."

Selene's worst fears had been realized. "What did you
do to her?"

While he remained silent, another round of mental
signals jumped into Selene's brain—Chloe in bed with her

eyes closed, Adrien pulling her into his arms, his hands at her throat…checking for a pulse. And following that, the sound of Adrien's mournful moan so full of abject pain, it took her breath.

A heavy blanket of sadness settled over Selene. "Did she take her own life?"

He paced the room a few moments before pausing at the window and turning his back to Selene. "I've already endured a coroner's inquest, Selene. I don't need one from you."

"I'm only trying to put together what happened."

"My disregard caused her death. That's all you need to know."

"Adrien, you need to talk about it. You've carried it around for so long it's destroying you."

He remained silent for a while before he finally said, "Fine, I'll give you the details. But it's not the kind of thing you've faced in your safe world."

"I don't care. I need to know."

He turned toward Selene, all his emotions on display, from his red-rimmed eyes to his remorseful expression. "Chloe was quadriplegic, paralyzed from mid-chest down, with some use of her right hand. She could breathe on her own, at least for a time." He began to pace as he continued. "The day before she died, I insisted she needed to move closer to a hospital so she could have more intensive care because she wasn't getting better. In fact, she was getting worse. She didn't want to go, but I forced the issue."

"And after that?" she asked when he looked as if he might clam up again.

Again he turned his back on her, as if he couldn't quite face her with the rest of the facts. "Ella took care of her during the day, and every night I read to her until she fell asleep. I stayed up and watched her to make sure she was okay. But that night…" He lowered his head. "I was exhausted and I fell asleep. When I woke up, she wasn't breathing. I tried to perform CPR, but it was too late. I honestly believed she gave up."

Her heart heavy from the utter sorrow in his voice, Selene set the papers on the bed and moved behind him. "How long did you take care of her?"

"For two years." Although he had yet to face her, Selene took the mental journey with him as he continued. "In the evening, I took her for walks along the grounds so she could enjoy some fresh air. She liked to draw during those times and even though she struggled, she still managed to do what she loved most. But it wasn't enough. I didn't do enough to keep her fighting."

Selene disagreed. Her opinion of him had only elevated because of his sacrifice. And now she understood why he couldn't sleep, the extent of his pain that she felt as keenly as if it were her own. In many ways, it was. "Not many people would have made that commitment to someone, Adrien. You thought you were doing the right thing. You *were* doing the right thing."

He spun around, stormed to the bed and swept the papers off onto the floor. "If I'd stayed awake, I could have called the paramedics. She would still be alive."

Selene moved in front of him and laid her palm on his face. "Or it might have only delayed the inevitable. If her health was failing, no one could predict how long she would have lingered on."

He sighed. "She deserved more time."

"She deserved some peace. When are you going to stop blaming yourself?"

"I can't."

She slipped her arms around his waist. "Yes, you can. You have to. I know Chloe wouldn't want you to continue to live this way. No one expects you to forget her, but she's asked for your forgiveness. Can you forgive her?"

He closed his eyes briefly and when he opened them, Selene saw a hint of tears he seemed determined to hold at bay. "I already have forgiven her."

"Now you have to forgive yourself. She had no choice but to let you go, and now it's time for you to let her go, too."

"What I did to her is unforgivable. I failed her twice."

She laid her head against his chest, relieved when his arms came around her. "Chloe forgives you, Adrien. And I forgive you, too."

He framed her face with his palms and forced her gaze to his. "Come away with me, Selene. Away from this place. I only have to make one phone call and we can be anywhere in the world you want to go in a matter of hours."

It would be so easy for her to say yes. So easy to disregard her responsibility to her family to spend time with him. But she'd made a promise to Hannah. "I can't, Adrien. Not now."

He took a step back. "You're afraid of me. You're still not sure I'm telling you the truth."

"I know you're telling me the truth. I have to go home for a few days to be with Hannah while she has her baby. We can go away after that if you'd like."

The coldness in his eyes cut Selene's heart to the quick. "Go. Be with your family. They need you more than I do."

She wasn't so sure about that. "I won't be gone more than two days, Adrien. I promise."

"No promises," he said. "Stay in Georgia, Selene. You don't belong here. You sure as hell don't belong with me. I'll only bring you down."

A deep ache radiated from her heart as tears threatened to cloud her eyes. "You don't mean that."

He turned and walked back to the window. "Yes, I do."

She tried to tune into his thoughts but received nothing but blackness. No emotions. No latent regret. Nothing.

"You want me to walk away from everything we've shared?" she asked.

"We shared our bodies and time. That's all."

Selene's eyes clouded with tears but she refused to let them fall, even if something deep inside her did. "Maybe that's all it meant to you, but it meant more to me. Much more."

As the world Adrien had shown her crashed down around her, Selene headed for the door, her thoughts a jumble of confusion. Yet before she walked away for good, she decided to make a last stand. "You know, I've wondered why I didn't stay in Baton Rouge that first night when I arrived in Louisiana. I've wondered why I kept driving even thought it was late. Why I stopped in St. Edwards and didn't bother to leave that following day, or several days after that. Now I know why."

He turned and stared at her, his face a mask of stone. "To save me from myself?"

"No. To love you."

"Well, you've really done it this time, Mr. Morrell."

Adrien looked up from where he was seated on the cursed hospital bed to meet Ella's scorn. "You shouldn't have let her in here."

"You gave me no choice." Ella strode into the room and sat beside him. "She had to know the truth, that you aren't a monster. She loves you, Adrien, and you should accept that love. Accept that you love her, too."

He didn't want Selene to love him. And he didn't want to love her, but he did. "If you knew everything about her, you'd probably be glad she's gone."

"If you're talking about her mind-reading abilities, she told me before she left."

He bolted from the bed and walked to the window. "That doesn't make any sense."

"It makes perfect sense."

That drew Adrien around to face her. "You're an intelligent woman, Ella. You know as well as I do that reading minds sure as hell isn't logical."

Ella folded her hands in her lap. "I've also lived in this culture long enough to know it's possible. I've seen it. And I knew the minute she showed up on our doorstep that she was different. That she was here for a reason, otherwise I wouldn't have hired her because of her lack of experience."

Adrien gritted his teeth and spoke through them. "Damn you for buying into this crazy concept of fate."

Her expression remained emotionless, even when she said, "And damn you for dishonoring your sister by wallowing in self-pity."

"I don't want to hear this, Ella."

"Maybe not, but you're going to listen." She pushed off the bed and stood face-to-face with him. "We both made mistakes with Chloe, not realizing the extent of her decline and possibly doing too little too late. But we had good intentions. Selene did, too. She forced you to feel something other than guilt. She made you realize you're still a man and not some hollow shell. You might hate that, but you don't hate her. In fact, she is a part of you now. Now I want to know what you intend to do about it."

What the hell could he do? He'd already screwed everything up, destroyed any chance of being with her because of stupid pride. "Nothing. I told her to leave and she's not coming back."

"She'll be back if you ask her to come back."

God, he wanted that. More than he'd realized until that moment. "I have no idea how to get in touch with her."

"Good grief, Adrien. You can find anyone if you so choose." Ella looked thoughtful. "Or if she can read your thoughts as she's claimed she can, then I imagine she'll be able to know how you feel without you saying a word, even if you don't make a conscious effort. You can't stop thinking about her, even now. And you won't stop torturing yourself until you can finally tell her that you've made a mistake. A mistake you can't afford to make. Otherwise you will truly be damned to a life of loneliness. And Chloe would despise you for wasting your life."

Ella left Adrien alone then to ponder her words as well as feelings so deep that he felt as if he might suffocate. He did want Selene with him. He wanted all the things that he'd denied himself, including the love that Chloe had made him promise he would find after she was gone.

His thoughts of his remorse over his role in his sister's demise had been replaced by a biting regret over letting Selene go. If Selene had been telling the truth, that she could read his thoughts, then she would soon know that she had not left his mind for a moment. And she never would, even if he never saw her again.

"He's beautiful, Hannah." Selene looked up from the perfect little boy cradled in her arms to meet her sister's prideful expression. "What are you going to call him?"

"Trey, since he's Douglas the third."

"He looks like a Trey." To Selene, he looked like an angel. *An angel.* Her thoughts immediately turned to Adrien. Her own fallen angel. She tried to concentrate on the future, not the past, as she ran her fingertip down the baby's downy-soft cheek. "I don't know how you're going to handle having a little boy."

Hannah smiled. "I've always been able to handle boys, sis."

True, Selene thought, and she only wished she had been as skilled with men as Hannah had always been. Or at least the one man who continued to play upon her mind and heart like a favorite song.

When the baby stirred, Selene stood and laid him in the bassinet next to the bed. "You should get some rest while he's still sleeping. You look tired."

"You looked tired, too. Feel free to sleep in the guest room, unless you planned on staying with Mom and Dad."

"I hadn't really thought much about where I'll be staying." It suddenly hit Selene that she had no place to go. No real home to speak of. "I can stay here and help out with the baby as long as you need me."

Hannah frowned. "What about your job?"

"It's over." As was her relationship with Adrien, and that made her eyes begin to blur with unshed tears, just when she'd thought she'd had none left.

Hannah looked alarmed. "Oh no, sis. You didn't get fired, did you?"

Selene pinched the bridge of her nose briefly to try and thwart the threatening tears. "In a manner of speaking, yes."

"What are you going to do now?"

"I have no idea." All Selene could consider at the moment was a hot shower and a comfortable bed, though she doubted she would get much sleep. "I'll think about it tomorrow, just like a good Southern girl."

"You were always one to procrastinate, dear daughter."

At the sound of the genteel voice coming from behind her, Selene's frame went as rigid as the bedpost. She turned to discover Lynette Albright standing in the door clutching an overnight bag, looking every bit the prosperous society queen in her chic white suit, not a blond hair out of place in her perfect chignon, though it was well past the dinner hour.

Selene forced a slight smile around her discomfort. "Hello, Mother."

Lynette looked appropriately appalled. "Hello? That's all you have to say to me after you disappeared without a word?"

An argument with her matriarch was the last thing Selene needed tonight. "Look, Mother, I'm tired. Right now I only want to go to bed."

"Selene's staying in the guest room," Hannah said. "And since she'll be here, you can go home to Dad."

Lynette gave Hannah a scolding look. "I will do no such thing. You might need help during the night with the baby."

"I'm breast-feeding, Mother. I don't think you can help me with that since the whole concept of wet nurses went out with the dark ages."

Selene stifled a chuckle in spite of what awaited her—a long overdue sit-down with her mother. "Why don't you and I have a cup of chamomile tea before we go to bed, Mother? Hannah could use a little bonding time with the baby."

Still looking somewhat disgruntled, Lynette said, "Fine." She pointed at Hannah. "Don't hesitate to wake me if you need a break. I can still rock a baby even if I'm not lactating."

After Selene and Lynette doled out kisses to Hannah and little Trey, Selene followed her mother into Hannah's small kitchen. While her mother retrieved the cups, Selene put on the teakettle, a heavy silence hanging over the room. That silence continued until they were seated at the dinette, teacups in hand, though much had been left unsaid between them.

"Tell me about this job, Selene."

Not a topic Selene wanted to broach, but she might as well get it over with. "Actually, I was restoring an historical home. But I'm finished."

Lynette raised a thin eyebrow. "That was certainly fast. I assume there wasn't much to do then?"

So much more to do, and Selene hated that she wouldn't

be finishing the job. Hated even more that she would never see Adrien again. "I basically got the ball rolling and now someone else will take over." Maybe another woman. Someone else for Adrien to seduce. Someone else's heart for him to steal.

"What are you going to do now?" Lynette asked.

Selene shrugged. "I thought I'd put that degree to use that you and Dad paid for. Maybe go to work for an interior-design firm. Or maybe even start my own business specializing in historical restoration."

"Jan Myers has a nice shop downtown. I'm sure she'd love to have you. Would you like me to call her?"

"Jan is an interior decorator, Mother. What I do is a bit more extensive." When Lynette appeared hurt, Selene added, "But I appreciate the offer. And if it's okay, I could use a place to live for a while, until I find an apartment."

Her expression brightened. "Of course we'd love to have you. Your old room is still in order."

"Thank you. I won't stay too long." Selene released a humorless laugh. "It's sad, moving back home at my age."

"You know you're always welcome. You can stay as long as you'd like." Lynette stared into her cup for a long moment before turning her attention back to Selene. "I suppose I should apologize for giving you such grief over the divorce. But I had such high hopes for your marriage to Richard."

Selene took a quick sip of tea to wet her dry mouth. "It was more of a merger than a marriage, Mother. We didn't make each other happy."

"I know that now. All I've ever wanted for you and Hannah is your happiness." She sighed. "I wasn't happy about your sister's marriage to Doug, but it didn't take long to realize how much they love each other. And that, my dear, is much more precious than all the gold in Georgia."

Finally, her mother had come around to seeing that a

man's worth wasn't directly related to his bank account. "I know what you mean about that kind of love," Selene said as she focused on the floral painting across the room. "A love so strong you can't catch your breath whenever he comes into the room. And even when he's gone, you miss him so much you physically ache. You feel connected to him, as if he's a part of your soul."

Selene looked up to discover curiosity splashed across her mother's face. "I had no idea you felt that strongly about Richard, Selene."

"Not with Richard, Mother, and that was the problem. I loved someone else that way at one time." She still loved him, still longed for him. Still suffered because of that love, though she would never take a moment of it back.

Lynette laid her palm on Selene's arm. "You'll know it again, dear. Anything is possible."

Selene wanted to believe in the possibilities but right then she couldn't get past her recent loss. "I hope so." She stretched her arms above her head then dropped her hands into her lap. "It's definitely bedtime."

"Yes, it is. And I'm afraid you and I are going to have to share a bed."

Selene scooted back the chair and stood. "I can sleep on the sofa."

Lynette came to her feet. "That's not necessary. We can manage in the same bed. I remember many a night when you'd had a bad dream and crawled in between me and your father."

Selene smiled with remembrance of all the nights her mother had lulled her back to sleep with soft lullabies and soothing words. How terribly wrong that she had forgotten. "I'm a little bigger now."

"Yes, but your father won't be in bed with us, either, thank heavens. The man snores louder than a steam engine."

They shared in a laugh along with a few recollections of wonderful days gone by as they walked to the guest room. Selene realized that although her mother had always been quick with her opinions, she'd always been the same when it came to comfort. And before they settled in for the night, Selene thought about Adrien's estrangement from his mother, the forgiveness that might never come, and recognized her relief over bridging the gap with her mother.

Before they turned down the lights, she gave Lynette a long hug. "I love you, Mom."

The joy Selene witnessed in her mother's expression warmed her heart, which had felt so cold all day in spite of the summer heat. "I love you, too, Selene. And I'll love you even more if you don't steal the covers."

"I'll try to be good."

After Selene turned down the lights, her thoughts again turned to Adrien. And as she drifted off, he was once more the last thing on her mind. The last thing she saw.

Selene...

The sound of her name, said in a deep, desolate voice, sent Selene upright in bed as she frantically searched the room. For a moment, she was disoriented in time and place until awareness settled over her like the mists that blanketed the swamps at midnight. She wasn't back at the plantation; she was at Hannah's. Her mother, not Adrien, occupied the space beside her. Yet she could have sworn she had heard him, but apparently she'd been dreaming. Until she heard it again...

God, I need you....

Even hundreds of miles away, Adrien had managed to encroach into her mind. Not only could she hear his words, she could feel his anguish as intensely as if it were her own. It was.

She could ignore his pain, or she could return to Louisiana and force him to acknowledge what she knew to be true—they belonged together. She could prove to him that she didn't intend to leave him, as long as he welcomed her in his life. By doing so, she could meet imminent rejection, or she could come face-to-face with her future. A future with Adrien.

A strong sense of purpose drove Selene from the bed and, as quietly as possible, she dressed in a pair of jeans and a T-shirt. Apparently she hadn't been quiet enough because while tying her sneakers, she looked up from her perch on the edge of the bed to find her mother staring at her.

"It's four o'clock in the morning, Selene. Where are you going?"

"Back to Louisiana."

"What on earth for?"

"To take care of something that needs my attention." Namely, Adrien.

Lynette tossed back the covers and slipped on her robe. "It can't possibly wait for a few days?"

Selene stood and grabbed the overnight bag, shoving in what she'd unpacked, which hadn't been much. Maybe she'd known all along that she wouldn't be staying for any length of time. "No, it can't wait. It's important."

"More important than your sister? Your family?"

"*As* important." She ran a brush through her hair and then zipped the bag before facing her mother again. "Remember that speech you gave earlier about wanting us to be happy? And the one about never leaving unfinished business behind that you repeated several times while I was growing up?"

"Yes, but—"

"No buts. Now is not the time to take back your motherly platitudes. I have some unfinished business and it could directly relate to my happiness."

Lynette frowned in her usual fashion. "Does this have something to do with a man?"

Selene piled her hair atop her head and secured it with a plastic clip. "Yes, it does. A man I love so much that I'm willing to fight for him. For us."

"I can't talk you out of this?"

"No, you can't. It's something I have to do or I'll never have any peace." She slipped the bag's strap over one shoulder. "Please tell Hannah I stopped being so cautious and that I love her and I'll try to see her soon. She'll understand."

Lynette looked as if she didn't understand at all. "How long will you be gone?"

Selene gave her a quick hug and a kiss on the cheek. "That depends on him."

"Does this 'him' have a name?"

"Adrien Morrell."

"Is he a good man, Selene?"

"Yes, he is. But he doesn't realize it. At least not yet."

Lynette groaned. "Don't tell me. He doesn't have a penny to his name."

She smiled as she backed toward the bedroom door. "He has lots of pennies, Mother. But more important, he has my love, and as you've said, that's worth more than all the gold in Georgia."

By the time Selene reached the plantation at noon, she relied on the support of sheer adrenaline and the prospect of seeing Adrien again to keep her going. She left her keys in the ignition and her purse in the front seat in case he again sent her away. Now if she could just hang on to her courage.

As it had been that first day she'd arrived, Ella took her time answering the summons and, when she opened the door, she didn't appear at all shocked to see Selene. "I've been expecting you," Ella said, confirming Selene's speculation.

Selene strode past Ella and into the foyer. "Where is he?"

"In his office. Where else?"

"Good. I have to talk to him."

"Did your sister have her baby?"

"Yes. A boy. I'll tell you all about it later." She hooked a thumb over her shoulder. "I need to do this before I lose my nerve."

Ella waved her away. "Of course. I have to warn you, though. He's in a foul mood."

"That makes two of us."

Despite her exhaustion, Selene practically sprinted into the rotunda and up the stairs, calling, "Yes, I'm back," at Demon Giles over one shoulder as she headed toward Adrien's office.

She paused at the door, her hand gripping the knob, while she took a moment to consider what she would say. A moment to prepare for the possibilities. He could turn her away, causing her heart to cave in once more. Or he could finally admit that he loved her.

Without bothering to knock, Selene opened the door to find the room practically absent of light due to the closed curtains. But the area wasn't so dark that she couldn't see Adrien seated behind his desk.

She immediately crossed the room and tore open the curtains on one of the windows flanking his desk. "Before you say anything, I know you told me not to come back." She moved to the other curtain and yanked it open. "But I've realized a few things in my absence."

She rounded the desk, braced her hands on the wooden surface and leaned into them while he simply stared at her. "First, as you've said, I don't work for you. Second, I signed a contract, one that you prepared, I might add, and I plan to adhere to the terms. I'm not going anywhere until I return this house to what it once was."

After drawing a quick breath, she continued. "And furthermore, I refuse to let you keep playing the role of tragic hero. Chloe's death was horrible, but it wasn't your fault. She made choices, tough ones, just like I'm making the choice not to give up on you, even if you've given up on yourself."

When he failed to move, or to speak, she said, "Well, what do you think about this so far?"

He leaned back in his chair. "Don't let me stop you since you're obviously on a roll."

"Yes, I am. And I'm going to stay on a roll until I make you realize that nothing is beyond forgiveness when you love someone. And I do love you, even if you don't love yourself right now. We're good together and I'm going to prove it to you. And if you think I'm being the belle from hell now, just wait. I'm not going to let up until—"

God, I love you.

His silent declaration came to her as clearly as cut glass. "Say it out loud, dammit."

He shoved out of his chair and turned his back to her.

I can't do this, Selene. I can't do this to you.

That sent her around his desk where she grabbed his arm and yanked as hard as she could, turning him to face her. "Yes, you can do this. You only have to be honest and admit how you feel." She clutched the front of his shirt. "Please, Adrien. I have to hear you say it."

When he remained silent, she tipped her forehead against his chest, unwelcome tears rolling down her cheeks and dampening the front of his shirt. His arms came around her and he rested his lips against her ear. "I love you."

She lifted her face and met his gaze, finally seeing the emotion that she had craved so strongly. "I love you, too."

He cradled her head against him and held her tighter for a few more moments before he leaned back and studied her eyes. "Belle from hell?"

She laughed through residual tears. "Yes, and don't forget it."

He kissed her then, first her damp cheeks and finally her lips. After a time, he broke the kiss and rested his forehead against hers. "What are we going to do about this?"

She leaned back and smiled. "There's nothing to be done. We'll just go with it and see what happens."

"You're taking a huge leap of faith, Selene, believing in me."

"I believe in us, Adrien. And I'm not trying to save you because only you can do that. But I can be there every step of the way while you heal. And you will heal, I know it."

He looked at her with so much love in his eyes that Selene fought back another rush of tears. "For the first time in a long time, I think you're probably right."

She held him tightly. "That means we can take up where we left off, spending more quality time together, getting to know each other better, beginning right now."

"I have to leave this afternoon. I'm going to Los Angeles."

Selene experienced the bite of disappointment. "Is this a business trip?"

"In part, yes. My offices are in California. I've neglected several important projects, including a foundation I've set up in Chloe's name with her trust monies. It provides funding for spinal-cord-injury research."

"That's a wonderful tribute, Adrien. I'm sure she would be pleased."

"Yeah, she would. I have to spend a few hours in Florida first. I need to see my mother."

Selene was more than willing to sacrifice some time with him if he was willing to restore his relationship with his mother. "How long has it been since you've seen her?"

"Almost a year. She came to visit Chloe a few times to

try to convince her to go home with her, but I made sure I wasn't around. We didn't speak at the funeral."

"Then I think it's past time to mend fences."

He pressed another kiss on her lips. "And I want you to come with me."

Considering Selene's sudden euphoria, he could have told her he planned to hand her the moon and stars on a silver platter. Make that a gold platter. "What about the house? The contractor should begin work soon."

"Ella can take care of that until we return. Is your passport valid?"

Her confusion came out in a frown. "Yes, but last I heard, you don't need one for California, unless it's declared independence without my knowledge."

"I don't plan to spend more than a couple of days in L.A. After that, we can go somewhere exotic. I'm thinking Barbados."

Selene was thinking she must be hallucinating. "You're going to show me that beach you've talked about." The one she had seen through his thoughts.

He thumbed away one rogue tear from her cheek. "I'm going to make love to you on that beach."

"I'm looking forward to it, but I have two conditions. First, I never want to have to delve into your mind to know how you feel about me."

"I promise to tell you often. What's the second condition?"

"That we get rid of that darn demon in the hallway."

Adrien's laughter was pure music to Selene's ears. "What do you propose I do with him?"

"Well, if you'd kicked me out again, I would have made a very improper suggestion on where you could stick him. But since you've been most accommodating, I believe we'll just have to carry him up to the attic."

Adrien swept her up into his arms. "We'll do that later.

Right now I'm going to carry you to my bed and make love to you."

"Now that's new and different, making love in a bed." Selene checked her watch as they headed out the door. "What time does our flight leave?"

"Whenever I tell it to leave. We have a few hours to make up for the twenty-four we've been apart."

"That's twenty-four hours and twenty-two minutes, I believe. But who's counting?"

He sent her a devilish smile. "I am."

When they reached his bedroom, Adrien set Selene on her feet and gave her a thorough and highly suggestive kiss before he gave her the softest of smiles. "I'm going to show you the world as you've never seen it before."

As far as Selene was concerned, in many ways, he already had.

They made love with the bright sunlight streaming into the open windows, leaving nothing undisclosed, including Adrien's sadness as he finally grieved in Selene's arms, something that was long overdue.

During those precious moments, when she glimpsed the man she'd known had existed all along, Selene knew that she never wanted to leave Adrien's world again. And she never would.

Epilogue

Two years later

Maison de Soleil. The House of Sunshine.

The newly restored Louisiana plantation had proven to be Selene Winston Morrell's first step toward freedom—and a blessed life.

The facade had been painted white and yellow, not a speck of black to be found. Inside, the downstairs chambers had been restored to their original grandeur, the nursery upstairs now a family room, and the room across the hall that at one time had been a place of sadness had become Selene's sanctuary—the office where she now ran her design consulting business.

Although the successful restoration had been one of Selene's greatest achievements, her most treasured accomplishment could be found coming out the front door in Adrien's arms.

When father and daughter strolled toward the picnic table set out on the front lawn, Selene stopped gathering the last remnants of the birthday party to survey the scene. With her cap of dark curls and her eyes as blue as the summer sky above them, the little girl looked so much like her daddy that it made Selene's heart soar from pure joy. A precious child that had been born almost a year to the day from when Selene and Adrien had spontaneously exchanged marriage vows on a remote beach in Barbados.

After stuffing the paper tablecloth into the garbage can, Selene rounded the table, knelt down and held out her arms. "Come here, Chloe."

Adrien set the baby on her feet and she toddled across the lawn as fast her newfound steps allowed, her curls bouncing in time with her gait, a vibrant smile splashed across her round face. Their fiercely independent child who was so full of life, much like the young woman for whom she'd been named.

Selene swept her up into her arms and rested her face against the crown of her head. "You smell so good, sweetie. Did you have a nice bath?"

"Between keeping her in the tub and getting the icing out of her hair and ears, that bath was a challenge."

Selene looked up to meet Adrien's smile. "Your efforts earn you five stars in the good-daddy department."

Chloe yawned and laid her head against Selene's shoulder. "She's definitely tired," Selene said. "But at least she'll sleep for Ella on the trip to Shreveport."

Adrien frowned. "Are we sure we still want to do this?"

Selene had to admit she was already missing her daughter, but she still believed they could use the break. "We've talked about it nonstop since Ella made the offer. It's only for a week, and we have to let her out of our sight sooner or later."

Adrien rubbed a hand across his neck. "Yeah, you're right. Did your family leave already?"

"Just a few minutes ago. Did you speak with your mother?"

"She called earlier to wish Chloe a happy birthday, and to ask if she could take Chloe for a day or two this summer. I told her yes."

"I'm glad." Selene had hoped her mother-in-law might come to the party, but at least Adrien had begun to communicate with her again, and she wanted to get to know her granddaughter. "Well, everyone has left except—"

"Come give your uncle Jeb a kiss goodbye, honey."

The request had barely left the man's lips before Chloe was wriggling out of Selene's grasp to head toward Ella's SUV.

Adrien came to Selene's side and slid an arm around her waist as they watched their daughter climb into Jeb's wheelchair, something else she had recently learned.

"She loves him so much," Selene said, a hint of melancholy in her tone.

"Yeah. He's definitely been a good surrogate grandfather to her."

"You know, in a way it makes me sad that she might not remember him after he's gone. But then that might be a good thing because it's going to be so hard to let him go when the time comes."

"We'll just have to hang on to the good memories." Something Adrien had learned over the past two years, much to Selene's relief. "You're absolutely right about that."

Adrien gave her a slight squeeze. "Besides, he's made it this long, he could last another five years or so."

Selene wanted to believe that, but she sensed that Jeb's time on earth might be coming to a close though he'd managed to stay around even after the restoration had been finished. And while she was pregnant. And after Chloe's birth. "I better go rescue him before your daughter chokes him to death with his own bow tie."

"Why is it she's always *my* daughter when she does something wrong?"

"Because that is the mother's law, according to me."

After sending Adrien a smile to counter his scowl, Selene walked over to the wheelchair and crouched beside it. "Chloe, don't chew on Uncle Jeb's tie."

Jeb rested a hand on the baby's head. "She's not hurting me, Miss Selene. In fact, she makes me feel like a younger man again. That's what new life does to a person."

Selene couldn't agree more. She'd quickly learned the healing power of a child, and of love. Although at times Adrien still withdrew, his moments of grief had lessened greatly since their marriage, and even more so since Chloe's birth.

Ella walked up with a large purple bag hanging from one shoulder. "Are we ready to get on the road now?"

"If you don't mind, Miss Ella, I'd like to have a private word with Miss Selene," Jeb said.

Ella lifted Chloe from his lap. "I'll just take the little one to say bye-bye to her daddy."

Chloe immediately curled her fingers into a wave and repeated, "Bye-bye."

Jeb waved back. "Live well, girl child. You are a gift to this world."

A lump formed in Selene's throat when she realized Jeb could be saying goodbye for good. While Adrien strolled around the yard with his daughter, and Ella loaded several things into the back of the SUV, Selene pushed Jeb's wheelchair across the lawn to the grove of pecan trees and stopped beneath the one that housed his childhood fort. After setting the brake, she knelt in front of him once more. "What is it, Jeb?"

He released a long sigh. "I spoke with Miss Chloe earlier today."

"I know. She's really starting to talk now."

"Not the baby. Mr. Adrien's sister."

Selene kept a calm demeanor despite her surprise. "Where did you see her?"

"In the place with all the angels while I was looking at her picture that hangs next to Miss Grace. She wanted me to give you a message."

Some might claim this was nothing more than the ramblings of an old man, but she knew better. "What did Chloe say?"

"She said thank you for bringing her brother back to life, for loving him and that she's going home now."

In so many ways, Adrien had returned her to life, too. A better life. Not always perfect, but pretty darned close. "I appreciate you passing that on."

He sighed. "I'm tired, Miss Selene. I'm ready to go home, too."

"I know. It's been a long day."

"I meant I'm ready to see my family in my glory home."

She laid her palm on his careworn cheek, her eyes misty. "I understand. But I'm going to miss you."

Jeb thumbed a tear away from Selene's cheek. "Now don't you cry for me, Miss Selene. I've had a good life, and you will, too. Take care of that baby girl and that man of yours. He relies on your love to keep him grounded."

"I rely on him, too."

"Of course you do, because it was his destiny to understand you. And yours to love him."

She stood and leaned to give him a long hug. "And I didn't ignore it."

As the warm breeze whispered around them and the locusts called to each other, Selene took her time wheeling

Jeb back to the awaiting vehicle. He'd become such an integral part of their lives that each parting had become more difficult for fear it might be the last time she enjoyed his presence.

But when she turned to him one last time, he gave her a wink and a smile. "Don't look so sad, Miss Selene. I don't know exactly *when* I'll be called home, so if I could have one more piece of Miss Ella's peach pie, I might be persuaded to make at least one more Sunday dinner. Or several."

Selene grinned. "I think that can be arranged in the near future."

While Adrien helped Jeb into the front seat and Ella stored the wheelchair in the rear of the SUV, Selene leaned through the open door to say goodbye to her daughter. She double-checked the car seat's strap then kissed Chloe's soft cheek. "You be good for Ella, sweetie. Mommy and Daddy will see you in a few days."

Chloe responded by popping her thumb in her mouth, her eyes looking as heavy as Selene's heart felt.

Ella slid into the front seat and shifted toward Selene. "She'll be fine, *shâ*. She'll have a good time playing with my new grand-niece."

"I know she'll be fine. But call if she's too fussy and you need us to pick her up. And be sure to call when you get there."

Ella presented her usual wily grin. "I'll call and let the phone ring once to let you know I've arrived, in case you are otherwise preoccupied."

Selene started to ask what she meant, but she already knew. And she did intend to be preoccupied with her husband for hours on end.

After giving both the baby and Jeb one last kiss and hug, Selene backed up and closed the door. She waved as she watched her daughter leave the plantation for the first time without her. But only the first of many times until she left for good to be her own person. At least that wouldn't happen any time soon.

Adrien circled his arms around Selene's waist and pulled her back against him. "I'm worried about her driving."

Selene looked back at him and frowned. "Ella's a good driver. Much better than you, in fact."

"I meant Chloe's driving."

She pulled his arms tighter against her and laughed. "Unless Ella's going to let her take the wheel as soon as they pull onto the interstate, I think we have about fifteen years or so to worry about that."

"It will be here before we know it."

So true, Selene thought. The past two years had practically flown by, yet she'd stored every memory in the haven of her heart.

After the vehicle disappeared from sight, she turned to find Adrien sporting a somber expression. "What's wrong, Adrien? And don't make me climb into that mind of yours to find out." Something she had promised not to do, and she hadn't, though he still tended to send out mental signals, especially when he wanted her, and that had been often.

"Nothing's wrong. I was thinking how much she would have loved you. How much you would have loved her."

Selene didn't have to ask who "her" was. "If she was anything like her brother, that's definitely true." She rose up on tiptoe and kissed his lips. "Now that we have a whole week of free time, how do you propose we spend it?"

"In bed."

She couldn't help but tease him a little. "Well, considering your daughter inherited your insomniac ways, we could probably use a few good nights' sleep."

He pulled her against him and kneaded her bottom with his palms. "That's not what I meant and you know it."

"I know no such thing because the only time we utilize the bed is to sleep."

He ran his tongue along the shell of her ear. "Okay, then let's go to the blue parlor."

She shivered. "We've been there. In fact, I believe we've been in every room at least once, if not twice since they were complete."

Adrien donned the look that had enchanted her from the moment she'd met him. "Have you ever made love against a tree, Mrs. Morrell?"

"Yes, Mr. Morrell. And I'd prefer the red room to bark burns."

"Then the red room it is." He grinned. "As long as you agree to something first."

"You know I'm always open to all the possibilities."

"Would you be open to having another baby?"

Since they hadn't really talked about another child, Selene was more than open to discuss it now. "I would not be opposed to having a son, especially if he looks like me since our daughter doesn't."

Adrien shook his head. "I prefer girls. They're much more interesting and complex than the male species."

"Adrien, you are anything but simple." He still retained that complexity, a riddle Selene might never solve, yet that mystery kept her on her toes, and their relationship as exciting as it had been since the day they'd met.

Following a down-and-dirty kiss and a few suggestive touches, Adrien said, "Why don't we take this inside and start on that baby?"

She squeezed his bottom. "Best idea you've had all day. You can play the tortured hero and I'll be the belle from hell."

"We can play it out however you want to, babe, as long we play."

As they headed into their house, arms around waists, Selene realized how very far they had come, from sullen sadness to easy laughter. From the shadows into the sunshine. As he'd promised, Adrien had taken her to special places, both outside and inside his private world. But most importantly, he had shown her his heart that had finally begun to heal, as well as the absolute power of love.

* * * * *

Hotel Marchand

Four sisters.
A family legacy.
And someone is out to destroy it.

A captivating new limited continuity, launching June 2006

The most beautiful hotel in New Orleans,
and someone is out to destroy it. But mystery,
danger and some surprising family revelations
and discoveries won't stop the Marchand sisters
from protecting their birthright…
and finding love along the way.

If you enjoyed what you just read,
then we've got an offer you can't resist!

Take 2 bestselling love stories FREE!

Plus get a FREE surprise gift!

Clip this page and mail it to Silhouette Reader Service™

IN U.S.A.	**IN CANADA**
3010 Walden Ave.	P.O. Box 609
P.O. Box 1867	Fort Erie, Ontario
Buffalo, N.Y. 14240-1867	L2A 5X3

YES! Please send me 2 free Silhouette Desire® novels and my free surprise gift. After receiving them, if I don't wish to receive anymore, I can return the shipping statement marked cancel. If I don't cancel, I will receive 6 brand-new novels every month, before they're available in stores! In the U.S.A., bill me at the bargain price of $3.80 plus 25¢ shipping and handling per book and applicable sales tax, if any*. In Canada, bill me at the bargain price of $4.47 plus 25¢ shipping and handling per book and applicable taxes**. That's the complete price and a savings of at least 10% off the cover prices—what a great deal! I understand that accepting the 2 free books and gift places me under no obligation ever to buy any books. I can always return a shipment and cancel at any time. Even if I never buy another book from Silhouette, the 2 free books and gift are mine to keep forever.

225 SDN DZ9F
326 SDN DZ9G

Name	(PLEASE PRINT)	
Address	Apt.#	
City	State/Prov.	Zip/Postal Code

Not valid to current Silhouette Desire® subscribers.

Want to try two free books from another series?
Call 1-800-873-8635 or visit www.morefreebooks.com.

* Terms and prices subject to change without notice. Sales tax applicable in N.Y.
** Canadian residents will be charged applicable provincial taxes and GST.
All orders subject to approval. Offer limited to one per household.
® are registered trademarks owned and used by the trademark owner and or its licensee.

DES04R   ©2004 Harlequin Enterprises Limited

Page-turning drama…

Exotic, glamorous locations…

Intense emotion and passionate seduction…

Sheikhs, princes and billionaire tycoons…

This summer, may we suggest:

**THE SHEIKH'S
DISOBEDIENT BRIDE**
by Jane Porter
On sale June.

**AT THE GREEK TYCOON'S
BIDDING**
by Cathy Williams
On sale July.

**THE ITALIAN MILLIONAIRE'S
VIRGIN WIFE**
On sale August.

With new titles to choose from every month,
discover a world of romance in our books written
by internationally bestselling authors.

Paying the Playboy's Price

(Silhouette Desire #1732)

by

EMILIE ROSE

Juliana Alden is determined to have her last—
her only—fling before settling down. And she's
found the perfect candidate: bachelor Rex Tanner.
He's pure playboy charm…but can she afford
his price?

Trust Fund Affairs: They've just spent a fortune—
the bachelors had better be worth it.

Don't miss the other titles in this series:

EXPOSING THE EXECUTIVE'S SECRETS (July)
BENDING TO THE BACHELOR'S WILL (August)

On sale this June from Silhouette Desire.

*Available wherever books are sold, including most
bookstores, supermarkets, discount stores and drugstores.*

COMING NEXT MONTH

#1729 HEIRESS BEWARE—Charlene Sands
The Elliotts
She was about to expose her family's darkest secrets, but then she lost her memory and found herself in a stranger's arms.

#1730 SATISFYING LONERGAN'S HONOR—
Maureen Child
Summer of Secrets
Their passion had been denied for far too many years. But will secrets of a long-ago summer come between them once more?

#1731 THE SOON-TO-BE-DISINHERITED WIFE—
Jennifer Greene
Secret Lives of Society Wives
He didn't know if their romantic entanglement was real, or a ruse in order to secure her multimillion-dollar inheritance.

#1732 PAYING THE PLAYBOY'S PRICE—Emilie Rose
Trust Fund Affairs
Desperate to break free of her good-girl image, this society sweetheart bought herself a bachelor at an auction. But what would her stunt really cost her?

#1733 FORCED TO THE ALTAR—Susan Crosby
Rich and Reclusive
Her only refuge was his dark and secretive home. His only salvation was her acceptance of his proposal.

#1734 A CONVENIENT PROPOSITION—Cindy Gerard
Pregnant and alone, she entered into a marriage of convenience… never imagining her attraction to her new husband would prove so *in*convenient.